P9-CLC-393

BEASTS
of
NO NATION

A Novel

Uzodinma Iweala

HarperCollins*Publishers*

HarperCollins books may be purchased for educational, business, or sales promotional use. For information, please write: Special Markets Department, HarperCollins Publishers, 10 East 53rd Street, New York, NY 10022.

FIRST EDITION

Designed by Matt Glassmeyer

Printed on acid-free paper

Library of Congress Cataloging-in-Publication Data
Iweala, Uzodinma.
    Beasts of no nation : a novel / Uzodinma Iweala.—1st ed.
        p.   cm.
    ISBN-10: 0-06-079867-X
    ISBN-13: 978-0-06-079867-3
    1. Child soldiers—Fiction. 2. Africa—Fiction. I. Title.
PS3609.W43B43 2005
823'.92—dc22

2005043343

06 07 08 09 ❖/RRD 10 9

FOR THOSE WHO HAVE SUFFERED

Je parvins à faire s'évanouir dans mon esprit toute l'espérance humaine. Sur toute joie, pour l'étrangler, j'ai fait le bond sourd de la bête féroce.

I was able to expel from my mind all human hope. On every form of joy, in order to strangle it, I pounced stealthily like a wild animal.

—*Une Saison en Enfer*

This uprising will bring out the beast in us.

—FELA KUTI

Acknowledgments

My thanks to,

The Kagan Fellowship Committee and the Mellon Program for their generosity.

My love and thanks to,

My advisor—Jamaica Kincaid—for everything. Your excitement, motivation, and guidance are much appreciated. Without you, this never would have happened.

My first writing teacher—Patricia Powell—for giving me the chance to explore and taking the time to show me what writing is about. Without you, this never would have happened.

My family—Mommy and Daddy for understanding and continuing to understand what this means to me. Onyi, Oke, and Uch for listening to my ideas (and tolerating my never washing the dishes). Uncle Chi-Chi and Auntie Uju for housing and feeding me for the summer. Uncle Chude and Dayo for keeping me on track with my work. Uncle Amaechi for the jokes and the *suya*. And to my grandparents and all of my other uncles, aunties, and cousins for their love and companionship.

Simi and Auntie Kaine for believing in me, taking care of me, and helping me to understand what it means to be from where we are from.

My friends—all of you who had nothing but good things to say without even reading a word of what I wrote. Nina for her unflagging support and for editing and proofreading up a storm (it's finally finished). Ian for being a huge role model (when I grow up, I want to be *almost* just like you). Adeline, Benita, Elliot, Robin, and Thenji for entertaining my thoughts (stay as you are forever). The Chateau for being there and for dealing with me (burn the videotape). And to Aaron and Ismael because you are who you are to me.

My agents, Jeff and Tracy—you are wonderfully kind and patient.

My editors, Anya and Tim—you are wonderfully kind and patient.

I am deeply indebted to all of you.

BEASTS
of
NO NATION

It is starting like this. I am feeling itch like insect is crawling on my skin, and then my head is just starting to tingle right between my eye, and then I am wanting to sneeze because my nose is itching, and then air is just blowing into my ear and I am hearing so many thing: the clicking of insect, the sound of truck grumbling like one kind of animal, and then the sound of somebody shouting, TAKE YOUR POSITION RIGHT NOW! QUICK! QUICK QUICK! MOVE WITH SPEED! MOVE FAST OH! in voice that is just touching my body like knife.

I am opening my eye and there is light all around me coming into the dark through hole in the roof, crossing like net above my body. Then I am feeling my body crunched up like one small mouse in the corner when the light is coming on. The smell of rainwater and sweat is coming into my nose and I am feeling my shirt is so wet it is almost like another skin. I want to be moving, but my whole bone is paining me and my muscle is paining me like fire ant is just biting me all over my body. If I can be slapping myself to be making it go away I am doing it, but I cannot even move one finger. I am not doing anything.

Footstep is everywhere around me and making me to think that my father is coming to bring medicine to stop all of this itch and pain. I turn onto my back. The footstep is growing louder, louder, louder until I am hearing it even more than my own breathing or heart beating. Step slap, step slap, step slap, I am hearing getting louder, louder, louder and then shadow is coming into the light from under the door.

Somebody is knocking. KNOCK KNOCK. But I am not answering. Then they are angrying too much and just kicking so the whole of this place is shaking and the roof is falling apart small small so that more light is coming in. And the wood everywhere is cracking until I am hearing PING PING and seeing screw falling from the door into bucket near my feets. The sound is fighting the wall, bouncing from here to there, through the net of light, until it is like the sound is pushing the door open so there is so much brightness. BRIGHTNESS! So much brightness is coming into my eye until I am seeing purple spot for long time. Then I am seeing yellow eye belonging to one short dark body with one big belly and leg thin like spider's own. This body is so thin that his short is just blowing around his leg like woman's skirt and his shirt is looking like dress the way it is hanging from his shoulder. His neck is just struggling too much to hold up his big head that is always moving one way or the other.

I am looking at him. He is looking at me. He is not surprising at all to be seeing me even if I am surprising for him, but his face is falling and becoming more dark. He is sniffing like dog and stepping to me. KPAWA! He is hitting me.

Again and again he is hitting me and each blow from his hand is feeling on my skin like the flat side of machete. I am trying to scream, but he is knocking the air from my chest and then slapping my mouth. I am tasting blood. I am feeling like vomiting. The whole place around us is shaking, just shaking rotten fruit from the shelf, just sounding like it will be cracking into many piece and falling on top of us. He is grabbing my leg, pulling it so hard that it is like it will be coming apart like meat, and my body is just sliding slowly from the stall out into the light and onto the mud.

In the light, my breath is coming back and using force to open my chest to make me to coughing and my eye to watering. The whole world is spreading before me and I am looking up to the gray sky moving slowly slowly against the top leaf of all the tall tall Iroko tree. And under this, many smaller tree is fighting each other to climb up to the sunlight. All the leaf is dripping with rainwater and shining like jewel or glass. The grasses by the road is so tall and green past any color I am seeing before. This is making me to think of jubilating, dancing, shouting, singing because Kai! I am saying I am finally dead. I am thinking that maybe this boy is spirit and I should be thanking him for bringing me home to the land of spirits, but before I can even be opening my mouth to be saying anything, he is leaving me on my back in the mud.

I can see the bottom of truck parking just little bit away from me. Two truck is blocking up the whole road and more are parking on the roadside. The piece of cloth covering them is so torn up and full of hole and the paint is coming off to showing so much rust, like blood, making me to thinking the truck is like wounding animal. And around all the truck, just looking like ghost, are soldier. Some is wearing camouflage, other is wearing T-shirt and jean, but it is not mattering because all of the clothe is tearing and having big hole. Some of them is wearing real boot and the rest is wearing slipper. Some of them is standing at attention with their leg so straight that it is looking like they do not have knee. Some of them is going to toilet against the truck and other is going to toilet into the grasses. Almost everybody is carrying gun.

The boy who is hitting me is running to the first truck. When he is reaching the door, he is bending down with his back so straight and his leg so straight. Only his head is moving back and forward, left and right, on his neck. Then he is standing up and suddenly, quick just like that, the door of the truck is swinging open and hitting the boy right in his big belly and he is just taking off like bird, flying in the air, and landing on his buttom in hole of water in the road. There is sound coming from all the other soldier. It is laughing sound.

I am lying here even if I am wanting to get up because my body is just paining me and I am fearing that if I am moving, somebody will be doing something very bad to me.

A man is coming down from the truck. He is looking like the leader. I am staring at the man and his jacket that is coming apart into many green string moving back and forward each time he is breathing in or out. He is wearing glove so dirty they are almost yellow or brown and his cap that he is holding in the sweaty place under his arm is flopping down because it is soaked almost all the way with his sweat.

I am watching him move from truck to truck. The truck is so old that the paint is falling off and the tire is so low that when he is kicking them, they are pressing in and out. All the other soldier is following each movement he is making; even all the one holding their gun ready to shoot is shifting his head to be watching him looking at every truck. He is moving slowly like important person to make sure that everybody looking at him is knowing he is chief. All of the other soldier is staring at him like he is king. I am staring also.

By the time this leader man is leaving the last truck, they are surrounding him and all of them are moving the same way he is moving. They are following him to me. Their shadow is surrounding me and their leg is like cage around me. Nobody is saying one word and the man is chewing the inside of his cheek just looking at me like I am ant or some insect like that. He is saying, so who is finding this thing? But nobody is answering.

Then he is saying louder, why is this thing here on the ground?

The boy who is finding me is now coming back from my shack with some banana just as black as the road. He is wiping fruit from his mouth with his hand and walking to this big man who is saying to him, Strika. Is it you who is finding this thing? And the little boy is nodding his head very hard like he is happy that the man is knowing it is him.

Enh! Strika? Is it you, the man is saying. Heyeye! Hmm! he is shouting and then he is turning to the other soldier and cursing them. So you mean of all of you GROWN MEN only this boy—one skinny little thing like this—is finding this thing here.

I am not moving and the leader man is throwing up his arm to the sky. He is shouting, where are you finding him, so hard that his voice is becoming high and sounding like it is sticking in his throat. Strika is pointing his arm at the shack. Is that right, the man is saying and shaking his head like he cannot be believing it at all at all. SSSSS! He is shouting, you. Where is Luftenant? Luftenant. LUFTENANT! And another voice is answering, he is in the bush.

The grasses is shaking and man is coming from there holding his trouser up with one hand and holding his gun with the other. His yellow skin is shining like gold and sweat is shining on his beard. He is running to us and stopping when he is coming to be looking at me like he is confusing too much. Then he is saluting very lazy, not like everybody else who is looking like they are not even able to bend anything.

Commandant Sah! he is shouting in voice that is even sounding like somebody whining. This man Commandant is saying, come here. Come here, until Luftenant is moving closer to Commandant who is shouting, JUST WHAT ARE YOU DOING? Luftenant is not saying anything. You don't know? Please Sah. I was shitting in the bush. And Commandant is grabbing Luftenant's ear until the man is squeezing his face with so much pain. Open your ear and listen to me well well, Commandant is saying. If you are wanting to shit, you are not shitting on my time. Who are you? Just running into the bush like woman. If you are wanting to shit, you should be shitting right here on the road. You are not leaving this road for anything. Are you understanding me Luftenant? He is nodding, yes yes, and all the other soldier are trying not to be laughing by stomping their feet and coughing or pretending to sneeze.

Can you be telling me what this is, Commandant is saying and pointing to me. Why are you leaving Strika to bring him out?

Oh God. What am I doing, Luftenant is saying. He is spy oh. It is ambush oh. Let's just kill him and clear from this place.

SHUTUP YOUR MOUTH, Commandant is shouting. Who and who is asking you to speak? Idiot. If anybody is coming here, we will deal with them proper.

Then everybody is starting to laugh, even Commandant, and while this is happening I am seeing how Luftenant is looking like he is wanting to be killing Commandant. He is grumbling to himself and making his hand into fist.

Commandant is kneeling next to me and smiling so I am seeing how his teeths is in his mouth anyhow, just yellow with gap here and there. His gum is black and his eye is so red. His nose is coming out into a very round bulb at the tip which is sticking over his fat brown lip. He is stretching his glove to my face, grabbing it hard but also soft like he is caring for me, and then he is looking at all of the blood, and dirt, and mosquito bite, and mud I am having on me from dragging in the road. He is clicking his tongue and saying to Strika, are you trying to eat this one or what. And Strika is shaking his head no. Since he is finding me I can never hearing this boy speak.

By now I am knowing who is Strika and Commandant and

Luftenant. But there are so many person who is just not saying anything at all that I am wondering if they are even knowing how to speak. Commandant is turning to me. Do you want some water, he is saying softly, but I am not answering because I am floating on top of my body and just watching. The world is changing into many color around me and I am hearing the people speaking, but it is like different language. I am floating away like leaf in water until KPWISHA! I am feeling cold and more wet and then how my body is so heavy all around me.

Strika, Commandant is saying. Go and bring more water. Strika is running to the last truck and jumping up. Then Commandant is saying to me, are you hungry? Are you thirsty? And because I am feeling much better and my head is feeling more clear, I am touching my belly and nodding my head yes.

He is saying, well that is no problem. If you are wanting food, you will eat. And if you are wanting drink, you will drink, but that is having to wait until you are telling me your name. How can I be sitting down to eat with a man who I am not knowing his name? Are you hearing me? I am nodding to him again, but word is not able to be coming from my mouth.

You are having name is it not, he is saying and sticking his face into my own face. I am trying hard to remember, to be squeezing my thought for my name, but I am not getting anything. Now Commandant is getting angry and pointing to himself. My name is Commandant. Everybody is always calling me Commandant. What is everybody always calling you?

I am shaking my head trying to remember as Commandant is just reaching to his belt and showing me one black gun like that. I am wanting to cry and I am feeling like I am having to go to toilet, but I am knowing if I am doing this, he will be killing me just like that so I am shaking my head and looking at his red eye until I am remembering just like that how in my village everybody is calling me Agu because that is what my father is calling me. I am whispering Agu, my name is Agu because it is hard for me to be talking and then I am seeing how Commandant is taking his hand from his gun and smiling. Agu enh? They are calling you Agu. Well, that is what I will be calling you, he is saying. And I am breathing again and my head is not hurting so much because I am thinking, Glory be to God in the Highest I am still living.

Commandant is having smile crawling slowly onto his face and he is turning to his soldier and saying, see this one on the road. Do you see him? And they are all shouting, YES YES while Commandant is touching his beard and using his fingernail to pick all the scab and cut from between the hairs. He is looking from soldier to soldier and everybody is staying quiet.

BRING WATER EHN! he is just shouting and Strika is handing him one small blue jerry can with red top. Commandant is taking one dirty handkerchief from his breast pocket and wetting it with some water. Then he is grabbing the back of my head and rubbing my face saying, well, if you are going to be eating with man, then you are having to be clean. I am feeling the water in all my scratch, bite, and cut and it is stinging me too much. I am wanting to shout, but he is smiling with his tongue in his teeths like he is finding and cleaning old treasure. I am so thirsty. I am grabbing the can, but Commandant is lifting it high into the air and pouring it onto my face and into my mouth. It is tasting of plastic and kerosene. It is having small small grain of sand in it, but I am managing. It is making me to feel somehow good.

Luftenant is snorting and stomping his feets. Commandant is saying to me, why are you just lying by the roadside like one dead rat. Luftenant thinks you are a spy. Is it so?

Luftenant is saying something under his breath and staring at me like he could be chopping me to many piece right there. So what is your business here, Luftenant is shouting at me.

SHUTUP YOUR MOUTH! Commandant is shouting at him. Who is asking you to be opening this your stupid mouth anyway? And then he is talking to me and saying, so what is it that you are doing here in one small small stall just waiting. You should be telling me. Are you spy? If you are not speaking, then heyeye! And he is taking one knife from its container on his leg. It is having black handle and black blade excepting the edge which is just shining so sharp it is looking like it can even cut hair right down the middle. The shine is blinding my eye and making me to fear. Otherwise, he is saying, I will just be giving you to Luftenant. Just look at him. I am not even knowing what he will be doing to you. Better you just tell me and I will be helping you.

I am blinking because of the sharpness of the knife. Looking at it is making me to feel like my tongue is cutting loose and just readying to say this and that. My father is telling me to run, I am saying to Commandant. Run far far so the enemy is not catching you and killing you. And then I am just hiding in the bush and running this way and that way not knowing anything.

Luftenant is snorting again.

Enh. Hmm. Is that so? Commandant is asking me. Where is this your father? And the other soldier is leaning forward until I am feeling like they are putting their eye on me, until their stare is just feeling like insect bite.

I am not knowing, I am saying and trying very hard not to be crying so these people are not thinking I am fool. He is saying that he will find me.

Commandant is sucking in his lip and touching my face softly softly. He is taking my hand and pulling me onto my feets. Do you want to be soldier, he is asking me in soft voice. Do you know what that is meaning?

I am thinking of before war when I am in the town with my mother and I am seeing men walking with brand-new uniform and shiny sword holding gun and shouting left right, left right, behind trumpet and drum, like how they are doing on parade and so I am nodding my head yes.

If you are staying with me, I will be taking care of you and we will be fighting the enemy that is taking your father. Are you hearing me? He is stopping and licking his lip. Are you hearing me? Everything will be just fine, he is saying with his lip so close to my ear that I am hearing his saliva in his mouth. I am looking and seeing his smile and feeling his hand on my face touching me softly. I am seeing all of the soldier with gun and knife and then I am thinking about my father just dancing like that because of bullet.

What am I supposed to be doing?

So I am joining. Just like that. I am soldier.

Luftenant is saying, don't think. Just let it happen. He is saying that the second you are stopping to think about it, your head is turning to the inside of rotten fruit.

Commandant is saying it is like falling in love. You cannot be thinking about it. You are just having to do it, he is saying.

And I am believing him. What else can I be doing?

They are all saying, stop worrying. Stop worrying. Soon it will be your own turn and then you will know what it is feeling like to be killing somebody. Then they are laughing at me and spitting on the ground near my feets.

We are stopping on the road and Strika and myself are just sitting in the back of one truck kicking the air with our leg and sweating with the sun. The wind is blowing softly in my ear and on my skin and I am looking at Strika and thinking all of the things I am learning as a soldier. I am learning to march, left right, left right; how to hide in the bush and stay very still so nobody can be seeing where I am, how to be walking one foot in front of the other so nobody is hearing me; running, jumping, rolling around on the ground and singing all of the soldier song that we are singing when we are working or marching. I am liking the older men and how they are carrying gun and always looking so tough like they are in movie and I am trying to be acting like them, but sometimes I am thinking of my home and my mother and father and sister and I am sadding. And I am thinking about Strika and asking myself why he is not even saying one word in this whole time I am soldier. If I am asking him question, then he is only shaking his head yes or no. So I am asking him all the time, even now while we are just sitting here waiting, are you Strika, and he is nodding yes. Are you having parent, and he is shaking his head no. Are you liking plantain? Nodding yes. Fish? Yes. Pear? Yes. Are you stupid? No. Why are you not talking talking? No answer. What is it like to be killing somebody? No answer. Strika! He is looking at me.

And then one scout they are calling Hope is shouting and running up the road. He is coming from the bush and yelling, they are coming oh! They are coming again! And as he is running he is tripping on himself running up the hill and all his muscle are moving even after he is stopping so he cannot be standing still. His gun is banging against his back like it is beating him to run faster, faster, faster, and I am laughing because he is looking not just like madman but mad horse.

Commandant is exciting softly softly when he is seeing the scout running for his life up the hill. Enh! he is saying and I am watching how he is folding his hand together and how his lip is just crawling to be smiling. Commandant is starting to sweating and I am seeing how his shirt is also soaking through with sweat. Luftenant is leaving him alone and looking like he is trying to find somewhere to be hiding. Commandant is thinking and I am liking to watch him thinking. He is putting his one hand in all of his big hairs and the other to be picking his beard and walking up and down backward and forward like he is in cage even if we are really standing outside in the open air. Then he is shouting order. Move this truck across the road! Park this truck here! Everybody take your position! You in the bush, speed up speed up! Quick. Quick quick. And we are all moving very quickly to do all the thing he is saying. We are causing so much confusion and chasing the small small animal from the bush onto the road. Lizard and bush rat and frog, they are all running and hopping and jumping. They are running around the road like chicken with no head just looking for place to be hiding. Strika is jumping up and down and grabbing his machete and then running to behind the tire of the truck blocking the road. I am following him because I am not knowing where to go, but I am putting myself behind the back wheel because there is not even enough space for two of us behind one wheel. Everybody is moving, rushing, jumping, hiding, and making noise until just like that it is quieting everywhere and it is only looking like truck is breaking down on the road. Even before the war, this is always happening, and now it is happening even more because war is making it very hard to be fixing anything.

I am sitting behind this tire, holding knife and waiting. I am watching mosquito everywhere moving around in circle like they are also waiting for something. If they are coming near to me, then I am beating them with my hand, but it is not doing anything. There are so many.

I am looking out from behind my tire and down the road the air is shaking just like still water if you are throwing rock into it. And then I am seeing small small truck moving closer, moving slowly slowly like cow. They are not even thinking anything is wrong and I am almost laughing and almost dying because my heart is beating so so fast and I am thinking about what is going to happen. They are not even knowing we are here and are just coming to us like idiot.

The first truck is stopping some meter from where I am hiding. I am looking around the tire into the eye of the driver. His window is shining with so much sun, but somehow is still looking dark. Next to him, one man with uniform is making sign. His face is scrunching up with fear and it is looking like his lip is pulling down all of his face, his nose, his eye, his eyebrow. They are looking at each other and then the driver is just disappearing behind the steering wheel. I am remembering the soldier who are coming to my village and I am holding my machete closer. I am liking how it is feeling in my hand, like it is almost part of my body. I am looking at the man and looking at Strika and I am saying to myself, if it is time to be killing, I am ready, but I am putting my hand between my leg because I am feeling like I need to be going to toilet. My heart is beating BUMP BUMP. BUMP BUMP. And I am finding it hard to be breathing, but still I am saying God will be helping me. I am ready.

I am watching.

The enemy is not even trying to fight and is just looking too tireding to even be thinking anything like fight fight, wahala wahala. Even if they are not yet seeing us soldier anywhere on the road, they are just jumping down from their truck looking like they are going to cry. PLEASE DO NOT SHOOT US! the man in the uniform is shouting. We are not having any weapon, or any food, or any money, or any ammo. ANYTHING! PLEASE JUST LET US GO!

I am counting them. They are only twenty, and they are looking like they are already dead. Blood is just covering all of their clothe and skin, sometimes even their eye, but I cannot be knowing if it is their blood or another person's blood. And they are even walking so slow like old man with walking stick.

The head man of the enemy is shouting, see. See. Our hand is up and we are not having gun. No weapon at all.

There is silence and then I am hearing Commandant shouting from the grass by the road, number one: This territory is belonging to all of us rebel. You are trespassing. Number two: Take off all your clothe and put them on the road. Number three: Lie down with your face on the ground and your hand stretching all the way out. If you are not doing this in ten second, we will be shooting you dead. Are you understanding me?

I am watching the enemy looking at each other and I am counting one, two, three, four, all the way up to ten, but they are not taking off their clothe. Then I am hearing KPWAP like one million people clapping and then KPWING when bullet is hitting the metal door of the enemy truck. The enemy is looking at each other and whispering until Commandant is shouting from the bush, COME ON! I SAID OFF YOUR CLOTHE!

EVERYBODY TAKE OFF YOUR CLOTHE RIGHT NOW!

Then the enemy is taking off their clothe very fast, just ripping the shirt and ripping the trouser and throwing it to the ground. Their body is just shining with sweat in the sun, and the mosquito is coming to them slowly slowly. Some of them are having underwear full of hole covering their thing and others are having to use hand to be keeping everybody from seeing it.

LIE DOWN! Commandant is shouting. Put your hand on the ground. They are lying down and I can see the tear on the face of one enemy. He is coughing and sniffling and whispering. I think he is saying, I am not wanting to die. Please God. I am not wanting to die, but I am too far away to be hearing him. I think this is what he is saying and I am looking at him and even feeling sorry for him, but then I am remembering my father.

Commandant is coming out of the bush smiling and sweating and holding his gun ready to shoot anybody who is not following his order. Behind him everybody else is coming from the bush from all side until there is not even any one place for the men to be running. Strika is coming out from behind his wheel so I am following him. He is collecting all of the enemy uniform and taking them to the truck.

The mosquito is getting closer. Closer.

Who is the leader, Commandant is shouting, but nobody is answering. He is walking up and using his weapon to touch the enemy who is talking first and begging begging PLEASE DO NOT SHOOT US! You. Where are your weapon? he is shouting. Get up. Where are they?

The man is saying, we don't want trouble oh. We don't have

any weapon. But Commandant is saying, Oho! This enemy dog is not wanting trouble, and everybody, excepting me and Strika who is never making any noise, is laughing, kehi, kehi, kehi like it is the best joke in the world.

Then Commandant is kicking this enemy man in the stomach very hard and the man is just dropping onto his knee and vomiting all over the ground.

Commandant is shouting, search the truck. Search the truck! and three soldier are running to search the truck. Then Commandant is telling me, Agu. Come here enh. Come here right now. And then he is telling the enemy chief to kneel down even though the man is already kneeling down and vomiting. I am standing in my place and I am just fearing. I am not wanting to be killing anybody today. I am not ever wanting to be killing anybody.

Bloody fool, he is saying to me. Come here and bring that machete. But I am still not moving. Commandant is stepping to me and grabbing my neck. You idiot, he is shouting. Come here! Come here right now! He is dragging me to the enemy soldier. Do you see this dog! he is shouting. You want to be a soldier enh? Well—kill him. KILL HIM NOW!

I am starting to crying and I am starting to shaking. And in my head I am shouting NO! NO! NO! but my mouth is not moving and I am not saying anything. And I am thinking, if I am killing killing, then I am going to hell so I am smelling fire and smoke and it is harding to breath, so I am just standing there crying crying, shaking shaking, looking looking. Then I am seeing, just like that, one enemy soldier is trying to run for the bush.

His thing is just bouncing up and down and his buttom is slapping until I am hearing gunshot and then seeing his flesh from his leg scattering on the road. He is falling to the ground but he is not even saying anything, not screaming or crying or shouting, but he is still moving, just dragging his naked body with his arm and one leg like he can still be running away. Nobody is even looking at him anymore, but I am hearing the sound of his moving and it is sounding like lizard scratching on the roof. I am shaking and holding my thing. I am wanting to vomit.

Nobody is moving. Commmandant is yelling, ANYBODY WHO IS TRYING TO RUN AWAY WILL NOT BE HAVING LEG TO RUN WITH. UNDERSTAND?

Please Sah. Please oh. We are not doing anything, the enemy man is saying from the ground and looking like cow because he is putting his hand for ground and just breathing like cow is making noise. Please Sah, and his tear is running down his face. They are mixing with his sweat and he is blinking so much. Please now Sah. Don't just kill us oh. Just take us. Make us POW. Please oh. We don't have anything.

Sah, one of the men is jumping down from the enemy truck and shouting to Commandant who is looking up from the enemy chief and watching the soldier throw down four gun, two big two small. They are opening up their hand to be showing that they are not finding anything else. Commandant's eye is flashing and he is slapping the enemy soldier with the back of his hand.

You are a LIAR! he is shouting and hitting him again and again and again. LIAR and idiot. Stupid somebody.

I am watching the man as he is just falling onto his hand and knee and spitting blood onto the road. Commandant is kicking him and I am hearing KWUD KWUD knocking inside my head. He is opening his trouser and pulling out his thing and saying to me, see Agu. See how we are dealing with this enemy. And I am hearing hsssss and seeing how Commandant is squeezing his eye and mouth and teeths while he is just going to toilet all over the enemy man.

Ahhh, he is saying when he is closing his trouser and everybody is laughing kehi kehi kehi. See this bloody goat. Get up you bloody fool! Kneel. Come on. Kneel.

None of the other enemy is even looking up from the ground. Some of them is going to toilet and making the whole air to stink. I am spitting because there is too much saliva in my mouth.

Kill him, Commandant is saying in my ear and lifting my hand high with the machete. Kill him oh.

The enemy is saying to me, please don't kill me oh. Please I beg enh. Please. God will bless you. And each time he is talking he is spraying saliva and blood everywhere. Then he is starting to piss and he cannot even be stopping himself.

See this man, Commandant is saying, look at him. He is not even man. He is just going to toilet like sheep or goat or dog. He is grabbing my neck and whispering into my ear, kill him now because I am not having the time oh. If you are not killing him, enh. Luftenant will be thinking you are spy. And who can know if he won't just be killing you. He is squeezing my hand around the handle of the machete and I am feeling the wood in my finger and in my palm. It is just like killing goat. Just bring this hand up and knock him well well.

He is taking my hand and bringing it down so hard on top of the enemy's head and I am feeling like electricity is running through my whole body. The man is screaming, AYEEEIII, louder than the sound of bullet whistling and then he is bringing his hand to his head, but it is not helping because his head is cracking and the blood is spilling out like milk from coconut. I am hearing laughing all around me even as I am watching him trying to hold his head together. He is annoying me and I am bringing the machete up and down and up and down hearing KPWUDA KPWUDA every time and seeing just pink while I am hearing the laughing KEHI, KEHI, KEHI all around me.

Then I am hitting his shoulder and then his chest and looking at how Commandant is smiling each time my knife is hitting the man. Strika is joining me and we are just beating him and cutting him while everybody is laughing. It is like the world is moving so slowly and I am seeing each drop of blood and each drop of sweat flying here and there. I am hearing the bird flapping their wing as they are leaving all the tree. It is sounding like thunder. I am hearing the mosquito buzzing in my ear so loud and I am feeling how the blood is just wetting on my leg and my face. The enemy's body is having deep red cut everywhere and his forehead is looking just crushed so his whole face is not even looking like face because his head is broken everywhere and there is just blood, blood, blood.

I am vomiting everywhere. I cannot be stopping myself. Commandant is saying it is like falling in love, but I am not knowing what that is meaning. I am feeling hammer knocking in my head and chest. My nose and mouth is itching. I am seeing all of the color everywhere and my belly is feeling empty. I am growing hard between my leg. Is this like falling in love?

Then I am falling down on the road and just watching as they are killing everybody, just cutting arm and using it to beat somebody else's head. And I am watching the man with his leg shot still scratching down the road as if he can be going somewhere. His leg is leaving trail like leaking car. And I am seeing mosquito everywhere flying in circle all around us.

I am not bad boy. I am not bad boy. I am soldier and soldier is not bad if he is killing. I am telling this to myself because soldier is supposed to be killing, killing, killing. So if I am killing, then I am only doing what is right. I am singing song to myself because I am hearing too many voice in my head telling me I am bad boy. They are coming from all around me and buzzing in my ear like mosquito and each time I am hearing them, they are chooking my heart and making my stomach to turn. So I am singing,

Soldier Soldier
Kill Kill Kill.
That is how you live.
That is how you die.

This is my song that I am singing all of the time wherever we are going to be reminding myself that I am only doing what soldier is supposed to be doing. But it is never working because I am always feeling like bad boy. So I am thinking, how can I be bad boy? Me, bad boy—somebody who is having life like I am having and fearing God the whole time.

I am learning how to read very early in my life from my mother and my father. When I am very small, before even my sister is born, I am always sitting with my mother on the floor of the kitchen and watching her washing all the plate. In the evening, I am always sitting on the floor just watching her with her buttom sticking high into the air and her breast touching her knee while she is working to make the kitchen so clean that not even fruit fly is wanting to put its egg inside.

I am liking to read so much that my mother is calling me professor. I am pulling her dress and she is saying to me, two more minute professor. Only two more minute. Then she is locking the door and holding my hand as we are walking to the main house. Inside, my father is always just sleeping sleeping or listening to his radio, so we would be moving quietly, getting the matches from the wood table in the middle of the room and lighting the lamp just in case they are taking the light. All of this is making me to agitate because it is taking so long until finally she is coming to the bookshelf and pretending to search for just the right book. The shelf was having many book of different size and different color—some red, some yellow, some blue, and some brown—but the one I am always wanting her to pick, the only one that I am wanting to hear is the one that is holding all of the other book up, the big white Bible. I was so small and the book was so big that I am almost not even able to be carrying it. But I was enjoying how the cover is so soft, and how the letter saying HOLY BIBLE was made of gold. This was my favorite book because of how it is looking and because of all the story inside of it. Whenever my mother is touching it, I am shouting, that one, that one and she is saying, shhh don't be so loud or you will be waking your father. I was always sitting in her laps on our favorite chair and we are staring at the small small letter on the page. She was reading over my shoulder and I am feeling her lip moving in my ear as she was saying each word. My mother is reading very very slowly because she is not schoolteacher like my father who is knowing too much about book. She is not going to school for long enough like my father, but she was always saying, I am knowing enough to read the only book that is mattering. This is why Pastor is liking her so much.

She is reading to me about how Cain is killing his brother Abel, and how God is visiting Abraham, and about Jonah living in the fish. She was also reading about how God is making Job to suffer very much, but how He is rewarding him at the end, and how David is killing Goliath. Each time she is reading this story I would be thinking in my head that I am standing here looking at how all the army is shining with gold and bronze in the sun and how Goliath is laughing until David is cutting off his head. I am seeing all of these thing when she is reading and thinking that I am wanting to be warrior. And all the time my mother is reading I am pointing to each word and asking what is that what is that so she can be telling me and I can be learning. We were doing this every evening until my mother is saying, okay Agu it is enough now. My eye is tired.

When my mother is not there, I was going to the shelf to be

reading The Bible myself. My mother was still reading to me every night, but I was also able to be reading by myself, and soon, when my father was coming back from work to be sitting in his short and singlet listening to the radio in his favorite chair, I was sitting with him and not my mother and I would be reading to him what I am teaching myself from The Bible. I was wanting to show him that I am big enough to be going to school so I can be learning everything that he is knowing that is making everybody in the village to like him so much. I was always asking him every day, tomorrow can I be going to school? Tomorrow can I go to school, and he was always saying to me, just wait just wait. Enh. Agu! Why are you wanting to grow so big so fast? Then I would be going to my mother to be begging her to help me go to school. I was wanting to go so much that each time I would be crying to her to make my father take me to school and she is saying to me that if I am crying like this, then at school they will just be laughing at me. So, when my father is coming home, I was first asking him how is his own school that he is teaching and then I was asking him if I am big enough and he was telling me to take my right hand and put it over my head to touch my left ear, but I was too small to be doing that so he was telling me, Agu you are not ready yet.

Until one day, I am running to my father and saying, look, and then taking my hand over my head and touching my ear. He is smiling and saying, okay, and then the next day we are going to the primary school where everybody is wearing uniform that is red short and white shirt if you are boy and red skirt and white shirt if you are girl. I was looking at all of them holding one red notebook and Biro in their hand and standing in line not making any noise. The boys were all having head shaved and the girls were all having plaits so that everybody is looking the same. I wanted to be wearing uniform and carrying red notebook and Biro too much so I was just standing there agitating.

My father was taking me to Mistress Gloria who is the head teacher and asking her if I can be going to school, but she was asking, this one? Isn't he too small? And I was looking at how Mistress Gloria is having very fat belly and big cheek and I wanted to be saying, I am only too small because you are so big, but my father is saying, no. He is not small and Mistress Gloria is having to take me in.

Because my father was schoolteacher and my mother is always reading to me from The Bible, I was already reading when the other children are just trying to learn. I was the smartest person in my class, so smart that the only thing I am having to learn is writing. Mrs. Gloria was seeing how smart I am and she is moving me up with the other people in primary one so I was just sitting on a bench with people bigger than me. When all of the other student are having their leg touch the ground while they are sitting, my own was just swinging back and forward in the air.

The school is just one big building with blackboard at the front of the classroom. This is where Mistress Gloria is standing when she is teaching lesson. All of the class are having their lesson in this one room so that Mistress Gloria was teaching every class up to primary six. She was always holding one large wooden ruler that she would be using to hit you on the head if you are not behaving well. Sometimes during the day we are having quiet time where the younger people is having to put their head down on their desk and all the older one is having to copy their lesson in their notebook. I am always doing my lesson at home so during quiet time I am sitting and thinking about different thing. I always liked thinking about everything that I am reading in book until it is time to play. Even though I am learning with the older children, I am always playing with all my mates. I am having one very good friend who is having Engineer for father so they are some of the rich people in the village. My friend's name was Dike. He was tall past me even if we are the same age, but he was still my best friend.

But these thing are before the war and I am only remembering them like dream. I am seeing my school and all of my friend. I am seeing Mistress Gloria and her curly black wig of hairs that she was always shifting around because it is not staying on her head well well. Some people were hating Mistress Gloria and always making fun of her by pushing out their belly big and walking around like fat goat, but I am liking Mistress Gloria and she was liking me. She was always saying to me softly when I was leaving the classroom after helping her to clean up, Agu make sure you study book enh? If you are studying hard you can be going to the university to be Doctor or Engineer.

All of this thing that she was always telling me are making me to happying because I was seeing how the Doctor and the Engineer is being treated. I was putting all this thing in my head and remembering them but not letting them be taking up too much of my time as I am young. So after talking with her like this each day, I was then going to play with all my friend in the schoolyard. I was having many friend in my village because all of the other children were thinking that I am nice boy and also I am the best at all of the game and all of the lesson we are learning. So they were all liking me and wanting to be my friend, but the person who was really liking me and who I was really liking was my best friend Dike. We are always doing everything together in the village. So after going from Mistress Gloria, I was going with Dike to be going behind the school yard with some of the other boy to be playing football in the dust with one flat ball that is never very good to kick or we are having the race that I am always winning and I was flying up and down the school yard even if I am only wearing slipper. I am liking school very much and always thinking about going until the war is coming and then they are stopping school because there is no more government.

I am always going to church every Sunday where I am first going to the Sunday school to be sitting outside under the shade of one big tree in the church compound with all of my mate and sometimes, if she is not causing too much trouble, my sister, to be listening to the women reading us more story from The Bible about Jesus and Joseph and Mary and telling us that we should watch out so that we are taking the hard road and not the easy road. And then we are saying prayer for forgiveness and the Our Father and also singing many song because God is liking music more than just talking so if we are singing, then He is listening to us well well. They are always telling us that God is liking children so much, that He is always watching us. Sometimes after

Sunday school is finishing I am going into the big gray church and sitting with my mother and father who are dressing in their nice clothe and listening to Pastor shouting and sweating. I am feeling how the wood is chooking my buttom with splinter and how the fan above us is shaking so much that it is looking like it was going to fall and be cutting off my head. I was always watching how the women would be dancing well well so that their clothe is shaking and they are having to tie it and tie it again and singing very loud when it is time to put their money in the collection plate. And the men are just shuffling their feets and bowing their head so their chin is touching their chest.

And on Sunday there are other thing that we are doing in my village. When there is no school and no chore, all my friend and me are making all kind of game to be playing. Sometimes, we are playing that we are grown up and doing grown-up thing like driving car and flying plane, or being Doctor or Boatman. And sometimes we are playing that we are soldier like we are sometimes seeing in movie and taking stick and using them as gun to be shooting at each other and falling down each time to pretending we are dead. And each time we are playing all this game we are having so much fun and laughing and running and yelling all up and down the road of the village. All the small small children are watching us and wanting to be like us and even the grown people are watching us and even if they are yelling at us to stop making so much noise, I am knowing from the way that they are shouting through their teeths they are trying not to be smiling because they are also wanting to be just like us. So we were playing all this game then and thinking that to be a soldier was to be the best thing in the world because gun is looking so powerful and the men in movie are looking so powerful and strong when they are killing people, but I am knowing now that to be a soldier is only to be weak and not strong, and to have no food to eat and not to eat whatever you want, and also to have people making you do thing that you are not wanting to do and not to be doing whatever you are wanting which is what they are doing in movie. But I am only knowing this now because I am soldier now.

So I am singing to myself,

Soldier Soldier
Kill Kill Kill.
That is how you live.
That is how you die.

And I am remembering to myself that I am doing all of this thing before I am soldier and it is making me to feel better. If I am doing all of this good thing and now only doing what soldier is supposed to be doing, then how can I be bad boy?

It is morning again, like all the other morning. The sun is just jumping up up into the sky so quickly that we are not even having any time before we are just sweating sweating everywhere. There are many tree around us, but they are all too far away to be giving any shade. I am crushing the grasses under my feet and just looking at how all of our footprint from the day before is everywhere. They are drying in the mud so it is looking like somebody is playing football here the night before, but I am knowing that this is never happening because nobody is playing football anymore during the war.

My feets is paining me. My leg is paining me. My knee is hurting because we are training very hard now. All the time just training training. They are telling us to run up and down so we are running up and down like we are running race when I am schoolboy. They are telling us to be crawling on the grasses and to be running zigzag to be dodging pretend bullet. I am hot and my body is too tired. I am not feeling good at all at all.

I am not liking this field even if Commandant is loving it

because he says it is taking away insubordination. I am not liking everything Commandant likes even if I am supposed to be liking it. But I am liking his shiny forehead and his big nose that is covering his whole face and even his top lip. I am liking his mustaches and his big black beard, and I am liking how he is squeezing his chin and all of its hairs in his fist when he is thinking very hard. I am wanting beard so I can be doing that. Maybe then I will be feeling older and I won't be tiring all the time. If you are seeing Commandant, you will be knowing that he is just very big man even though this war is coming to make most men small like children and children small like baby. He is so tall that looking at him is like climbing tree, so big that if he is standing next to you, then his shadow is blocking the sun. He is so strong that I can be seeing the vein on his arm. It is funny to be watching him moving also because he is walking like his leg is wooden pole that is not bending for anything. Before the war, this how I am seeing soldier moving when they are parading in the town near my village so I am knowing he is real soldier. Even when we are running his leg are moving this way and it is making me to want to laugh at him, but nobody is laughing at him because that is annoying him. He is beating people who annoy him and one time he was even killing one man who just annoyed him too much. We are leaving that man somewhere on the roadside with one big hole in his head and his eye wide open.

As we are standing in this field, Commandant is walking in front of us and shouting, are we soldier? We are saying, yes Sah! Are we army? Are we strong and proud? And we are saying, yes Sah! Yes Sah! and he is smiling, but I am knowing that he is not believing what we are saying because sometimes he is talking to himself that we are hopeless and only good enough to be thrown into battle and die.

I am not knowing why he is so angry with us all of the time for not acting like real soldier. We are not even looking like real soldier. There are almost one hundred and twenty of us standing at attention, but none of us is even wearing the same dress. Some of us is wearing green camouflage like real soldier are doing, but our own is just fulling with hole and having thread just blowing this way and that in the wind. If we are killing soldier or finding it on any dead body, then person is always quarreling and sometimes even fighting to be stealing it. Other soldier is wearing black trouser and black shirt with red stripe on the arm which is the uniform that the police is wearing before the war. This uniform is not as good because it is making you too hot in the sun and it is making you too easy to see in the daytime, but that is not mattering to anybody. People are just wanting to wear anything that is looking like uniform. I am not even having one uniform because I am too small. I am just wearing my short and shirt that I am taking from village we are looting one day. I was really wanting trouser to be stopping the mosquito from biting me on the leg, but I am not finding any small enough for me to be wearing. Anyway, I am really liking my shirt even if it is dirty and I am having to fold the sleeve a whole six time. I am liking it even if it is too big so it is coming down over my short.

Sometimes I am thinking, if army is always having one uniform for its soldier to wear, and we are not all wearing the same uniform, then how can we be army. And if army is made of soldier and we are not army, then how can we be real soldier. This is why I am not knowing why Commandant is always so angry with us.

Commandant is saying we are going to raid one village. Where is the village, I am asking to myself. And what are we to be taking from them? I am not knowing, but I am not going to be asking or he might be beating me. Then he is saying to us if we are hating the enemy and each time we are answering, YES SAH! We are stomping the ground and sometimes even jumping up in the air. He is saying to us if the enemy is killing our mother and our father and burning our house and we are answering softly, yes Sah, because we are all thinking of all the place and person we are leaving behind. I am thinking of my mother and my sister who are running away. I am not knowing if they are dead or alive or if I can even be knowing what they are looking like if I am seeing them today. Every time we are seeing woman or girl, I am looking at them well well to be knowing if they are my mother or my sister.

Commandant is shouting at us to be ready for fourteen hundred hours. I am thinking that this is very funny and I am wanting to laugh. Everybody is knowing that the day is not having fourteen hundred hours and I am looking down the line of soldier to see if Strika is also thinking it is funny. He is leaning forward to look at me, sticking out his tongue and opening his mouth wide. I am wanting to laugh, but instead I am sucking in my belly and holding my breath. Commandant is raising his head high until his face is shining like it is made of metal. DISMISSED! he is shouting at us and then he is walking off to the tree and the path that is leading to the many hut we are living in.

Some of the men are following Commandant, swinging their gun onto their back and walking quietly quietly. Some of these soldier, everything he is doing, they are doing. Everything he is saying, they are doing. Some other men is holding their gun by the front and letting the end to be dragging in the ground like plow when the men is going to find shade to be resting in. I am going to find Strika.

I am finding him sitting under tree far away from the other men, holding stick and scratching picture into the dry ground. Over and over again he is drawing the same picture of man and woman with no head because their head is rolling away on the ground. Strika, I am calling to him, and he is looking up at me. No noise from him. He is not saying anything, I am telling myself. Since I am becoming soldier, I am never hearing the sound of his voice, but now, I am knowing what is his problem. His picture is telling me that he is not making one noise since they are killing his parent. I am not believing him the first time he is telling me this, and every time I am trying to get him to say something or at least be making one sound from his mouth. I am feeling sad for him. I am getting used to it; this is how he is behaving from the very beginning. Strika is moving to one side so I can also be sitting in the shade next to him. Because I am tall more than him, I am knowing that I am older, but nobody is really telling how old they are anymore. All we are knowing is that, before the war we are children and now we are not. I am looking at Strika and how his skin is just brown in some place and black in other place, looking just like camouflage dress everybody is wearing. I am laughing when I am seeing him and

BUSINESS REPLY MAIL

FIRST-CLASS MAIL   PERMIT NO. 96   RADNOR PA

POSTAGE WILL BE PAID BY ADDRESSEE

PO BOX 5530
RADNOR PA 19088-5531

BIGGER, BOLDER, and BETTER!

← 10-1/2" →

← 8" →

Summer TV's Top 10 Guilty Pleasures

JULY 10-16, 2006 $1.99

TV GUIDE

STARGATE
Previews of
SG-1 and
Atlantis

ENTOURAGE
What's Next
for Ari?

THE OFFICE
The Ultimate
Insider's Guide

PROJECT RUNWAY EXCLUSIVE

HEIDI KLUM

On the new season,
her marriage & being a
mom for the third time!

← *Best Deal!* **SAVE OVER 70%!**

☐ **Yes!** Send me 54 issues for just 59¢ an issue billed in 4 monthly
payments of $7.89 each – a savings of 70%* off the cover price.

☐ Send me 27 issues for just 71¢ an issue billed in 4 monthly
payments of $4.79 each – a savings of 64%* off the cover price.

NAME _____ (PLEASE PRINT)

ADDRESS _____

CITY _____ STATE _____ ZIP _____

NTA710A0T

Send No Money Now!

TV GUIDE

saying to him, ha ha. Kehi kehi kehi. Strika is looking like shirt.

On the ground he is writing HUNGRY and I am wanting to say to him, I am hungry too. I am hungry too, but the word are not coming out of my mouth. There is no food left for anybody in the camp. Strika is putting his head on my leg and licking his cracking lip. The blood on them is dry and shiny, making his lip to look like he is swallowing red paint. I am touching his forehead with my hand and then I am touching my own to be seeing if he is hotter than me, but we are the same hotness. He is not having fever and I am not having fever. We are just tired. Strika is punching the air above his head. We are not wanting to fight. We are tired of fighting. I am saying to him, one day there will be no more war and we can be living together in a house and eating all of the food we are wanting to eat. Are you hearing me? He is not acting like he is hearing anything I am saying because he knows it is lie. We will always be fighting war, but sometimes it is nice to be thinking that there is something else for our future.

Luftenant is shouting, IT IS FOURTEEN HUNDRED HOURS, and I am hearing the voice of Commandant saying, come on! Get ready! Time to go. Time to go.

And then we are loading the truck on the road near to our hut and building. Even the truck is not wanting to go. They are not sounding good at all at all. The engine is coughing and spitting like sick old man. The back of the truck is having long wooden seat that is chooking you with splinter if you are even luckying enough to getting seat. And, if you are not luckying, then when the truck is moving, your head is moving from side to side with the bump in the road and you are feeling like you have been in battle before the killing even starts. Commandant is having smaller truck for himself which I am liking better because it is giving more comfort. Sometimes, if we are making him to happy, he is taking Strika and me to be riding in, but this is only sometimes. Most of the time, we are having to ride in the big truck with the other soldier.

Commandant is dividing people like this, you. Come with me. You, go with Luftenant. You come with me. You go with Luftenant. I am standing next to Strika when he is putting person here and there because I am wanting to be in the same group as Strika. And also I am wanting to be in the same group as Commandant because he is real soldier and making people to behave more like soldier than Luftenant. Commandant is choosing. One of the people he is taking is Strika and one of the person he is not taking is me. I am wanting to be with Strika and Commandant, but of course the thing you are wanting most is always the thing that is not happening. I am not wanting to be with Luftenant and I am not wanting to ride in his truck.

I am not liking Luftenant because he is coward. I am knowing he is coward because his skin is looking very light and yellow like one of his parent is white man. I am not knowing if it is his mother or father that is white because, most of the time, I am wondering if he is even having mother or father. One time I am hearing him say that before the war he is selling shoe, but that is only because he is not having chance to go to school; and I am hearing him say also that his mother and his father are dying in car crash when he is young and that is how he is ending up selling

shoe in the market. I am not believing him and I am thinking that
no other soldier is believing him. I think he is being born to sell
shoe and that he is only Luftenant of rebel because he is bribing
somebody to be giving him this rank. I am knowing it because
one day after Commandant is abusing him for not fighting, I am
hearing him grumbling that he is becoming Luftenant because
he is thinking that officer is not having to fight. Whenever he is
near Commandant, he is acting like one scared dog and not even
speaking. And in battle, he is never coming to the front and
always staying at the back where he is trying to tell people what
to be doing. Always, he is hiding behind the truck or anything
that is giving him protection from the bomb and the bullet. I am
even seeing him use dead body for protection, but I am also seeing other people doing the same thing so I am not too angry
about that. Still, I am not wanting to be with Luftenant because
I am fearing that I will be dying too quickly and then I will never
be seeing my family again.

I am angrying that Commandant is not taking me and Strika
together and I am fighting very hard to get into the back of
truck first so at least I am not having to stand and be too too
tired wherever we are going to raid. I am finding my seat in the
corner where I am having wood wall on one side. This way no
one can be pushing me this way or that way. No one will be making me to get up.

The road is going on and on. I am looking through the
wooden board to where the tree is moving by like it is running and
I am seeing the road, which is moving like black river carrying

us to far away. I am feeling the cold air on my body that is push-ing away all the heat from all of the body on this truck so I am not sweating as much. And my head, it is moving from side to side so much that I am having to use my hand to be holding it in one place. Hunger is attacking me because I am not eating any-thing since so long. Sleep is attacking me because the truck is just rocking back and forward and back and forward with all of the bump in the road. Sleep is attacking me and I am beginning to think of my village. It is so long since I am even seeing it in my dream.

All the truck is stopping. We are here at one junction and everybody is getting down, but I am the last to get down because I am the first to be sitting in the truck. As soon as I am jumping down into the outside, I am starting to sweating and it is sticking to my skin like million shiny insect. I am brushing the sweat away, but it is only making my hand wet and to be smelling like wet mud. Everybody is stretching his body this way and that way and Commandant is shouting to us, THE BLOOD MUST FLOW!, and we are all saying back, YES SAH!

Commandant is walking up and down and folding his hand one on the other and just looking around. He is putting his hand in his hairs and also holding his beard and this is making me to fear somehow. I am wondering if he is knowing where we are going or how we are going to be getting there.

I am looking behind me down this hill at the land that is stretching for kilometer and kilometer. Everything is green because this is the South of the country and we are having many tree. These tree are very fat because they are having so much water to drink. From the top of this hill, I am seeing through the tall grasses by the roadside to where the land is meeting the sky. I am not knowing where the hill is stopping or the bottom of the cloud is beginning because it is so far away that all of this is happening. I am seeing many many tree, too many tree that it is making me to wonder if God is planting all of the tree He can think of in this part of the country. Maybe He is running out before He is getting to the North where Government is and this is why they are angrying at us and wanting to kill us, because God is forgetting them. From this hill it is looking like you can just be jumping into the top of the tree for them to catch you, but I am knowing that that cannot happen. One day one soldier from our group is jumping off tall rock because he is saying he is finding heaven in all of the tree. I am thinking that he was madding in the head. I am not knowing if he is finding heaven, but I am not wanting to try it for myself to be finding out.

Nobody is telling me the name of these tree, so I am making it up. I am only knowing the Iroko tree, so I am calling those one when I am seeing them. But some of the tree are shorter than the Iroko tree and I am calling these one the children of the forest. There are tree with leaf that are having five point, so I am calling them the star-leaf tree because it is like their leaf is becoming the star in the sky when they are falling. I know because when this leaf is falling to the mud, it is becoming yellow like the color of star. And there is some smaller tree with vine that is strangling them. I am calling these tree the slave tree because they are slave to the vine that is using them to climb up to the sun. If I am tree, then I will be liking to be like the Iroko because they are so tall and strong that nothing is bothering them, but I am thinking that I am more like slave tree because I can never be doing what I want.

I am not wanting to fight today because I am not liking the gun shooting and the knife chopping and the people running. I am not liking to hear people scream or to be looking at blood. I am not liking any of these thing. So I am asking to myself, why am I fighting? Why can I not just be saying no? Then I am remembering how one boy is refusing to fight and Commandant is just telling us to jump on his chest, so we are jumping on his chest until it is only blood that is coming out of his mouth.

Commandant is saying, form rank. You who are going with me and you who are going with Luftenant. We are forming them but they are not even straight. My leg is shaking shaking. Everybody's leg is just shaking shaking because nobody is liking to be standing on the main road like that. Even Commandant is fearing because he is turning his head from side to side and looking down the road one way and then up the road the other way. He is looking up to the sky and I am knowing that he is thinking about how government is sometimes flying plane or helicopter to be dropping bomb and fire on everybody. He is speaking very fast when he is shouting, TENSHUN!, and we are all shouting back, YES SAH! This village is between these two road, he is shouting, so people with me will be attacking from one end when people with Luftenant is attacking from the other. That

way there is not even any place for these dog to be running. We
will be killing them like they are killing us and we will be stealing from them what they are stealing from us. We are shouting
back to him, YES SAH!

He is taking his people, one of them is Strika, but he is leaving me to be going with Luftenant and Rambo. I am liking
Rambo and wanting to be wearing red bandanna like that on my
head like he is wearing to be keeping the sweat from pouring
into his eye when he is busy killing killing. Nobody is knowing
why he is getting the name Rambo, but I am knowing of the
movie and how that man is very tough and mean and I am thinking to myself, yes, yes this Rambo is very tough and also mean,
but he is also very smart. I am liking the way his eye is so sharp
that they are seeing everything each time we are in battle. He is
dodging bullet and bomb and all of the thing that are killing people. Sometime I am wondering if he is having his own juju to be
making him live without fearing death, but I am not wanting to
ask him or he will be laughing at me. I am knowing that if I am
staying with him, then at least I am surviving, so it is not making me to feel too so mad that I am having to go with Luftenant
this time.

There is not enough gun for each person to be having one
and so I am not having gun. Anyway, Commandant is saying
that I am too small to be carrying gun because small person is
not holding gun well well and just bouncing up and down when
they are shooting. Instead he is giving me knife. But everybody
is getting gun juice. Everybody is always wanting gun juice
because it is drug and making life easy easy. Gun juice is making

you to be stronger and braver. It is making your head to hurt and it is tasting like bullet and sugarcane. I am not liking how it is the color of oil and the color of black paint or water in the gutter, but I am struggling to get my own so I can be putting it in my mouth. It is tasting like licking rock and it is tasting like eating pencil, but it is also tasting like licking sweet. My throat is burning like the fire of gun, but it is also sweeting like sugar cane. I am wanting more gun juice.

My belly is growling like hungry dog because the gun juice is making it to be that way. I am feeling hungry and I am not feeling hungry. I am wanting to vomit and I am not wanting to vomit, but I am thinking, let me not be vomiting because I am not even eating very much food so if I am vomiting there is nothing staying inside my stomach to be giving me energy.

Commandant is shouting, but I am hearing him like he is speaking through one big bag of cotton. He is saying, let us pray, let us pray and then he is asking the Lord to be guiding us in everything we are about to be doing. I am thinking that we should not even be asking God for anything because it is like He is forgetting us. I am trying to forget Him anyway even if my mother would not be happying with me. She is always saying to fear God and to always be going to church on Sunday, but now I am not even knowing what day is Sunday. I am saying bye to Strika and watching him walking away with Commandant. I am just waiting for the gun juice to start to working so I am not having to think as much anymore.

We are walking down into the valley and down into the bush so I am feeling like animal going back to his home. My forehead is heating up and my hand is hot and I am finding it hard to be breathing like the air is water, like in the place the cloud is borning before they are bringing rain. I am hearing water and I am thirsty and wanting to drink, but the stream we are coming to is having too much mud. Anyway, it is not mattering. I am putting my head in the water and when I am bringing it out the sky is many different color and I am seeing spirit in the cloud. Everybody is looking like one kind of animal, no more human. Nobody is having nose or lip or mouth or any of the thing that is making you to remember somebody. Everything is just looking like one kind of animal and smelling like chicken or goat, or cow.

Across the stream, I am feeling in my body something like electricity and I am starting to think: Yes it is good to fight. I am liking how the gun is shooting and the knife is chopping. I am liking to see people running from me and people screaming for me when I am killing them and taking their blood. I am liking to kill.

Across the stream, I am feeling like man with big muscle and small head and I am thinking that nothing can be stopping me and nothing can be slowing me down—not even the hill we are climbing. I am like leopard hunting in the bush and I am feeling like I am going home.

All of the leaf is red and dripping and all of the plant is too thick. The bush is chooking me with its branch and it is trying to trip me with its root, but I am running running through all of the color of this world, through all the tree, through all the flower. If I am falling on my knee it is not mattering because I am getting up and running, running, running. Nobody is knowing we are coming here, coming just like cloud when you are not even expecting it.

On the path, I am feeling wet mud between my toe and the grasses like knife on my ankle. I am saying prayer to God but all my word is going to Devil. Help me to be doing the thing You want me to do, I am saying, but I am only hearing laughter all around me in the tree and in the farm we are passing, many farm that is having no more yam or cassava because there is nobody staying to be growing them.

And on the path, we are coming to the edge of this village where there are the poor person house made of mud and tin and wood. There is nobody living inside so we are tearing them down and setting the thatch roof on fire and then we are moving on to more house. Each person is taking house and saying, this is my house and everything that is in it is belonging to me. I am running to the smell of smoke in one house that is having wall of cement with breaking-up glass on top to be keeping away the terrible people like Commandant and Luftenant.

Person in this house is trying to keep safe behind iron gate, but we are pushing it pushing it until it is opening with big scream like it is not wanting to be opening at all at all. There is soft dirt under my feets and tall green tree with orange and mango. Every building here is painting green even if it is fading, but they are rising from the grasses with white window like bone inside them.

Far away, I am hearing screaming and gunfire and my head is growing smaller and my body is growing bigger. I am wanting to kill; I don't know why. I am just wanting to kill. I am seeing animal and I am wanting to kill it. I am raising my machete and then I am seeing. I am shouting, STRIKA! because I am almost chopping him. He is looking like dog to me, but we are hugging in all of the screaming and the gunfire and I am feeling his head and he is feeling my head and then we are going together through all of the changing color to the main house of this compound.

In the main house, there is no food, nothing to lick, nothing to chop, nothing. Breaking glass is everywhere like someone is coming here before. All of the chair is breaking, but there is still picture on the wall, and there are plastic flower lying on table.

So many door from this room. They are leading down hallway. The smell of shit and piss is all around us. At the end of the hall, soldier is breaking down door, KPWAMA, KPWAMA, they are kicking and knocking it with machete until the wood is breaking.

In the room, I am looking up and seeing—sky. There is nothing to be keeping out the rain or God from watching what it is we are doing. The sun is coming loose like someone is cutting it and it is bleeding red and yellow and purple and blue above us. In the corner, there is desk being eaten by termite and in the other corner is bed smelling like chicken and goat. I am wanting to kill. We are all wanting to kill.

Under the bed there is woman and her daughter just hiding. She is looking at us and worrying worrying so much it is looking like somebody is cutting her face with knife. She is smelling like goat and we are wanting to kill her so we are dragging her out, all of us soldier, but she is holding her daughter. They are holding each other and shaking like they are having fever. They are so thin more than us and the skin is hanging down like elephant skin so I am knowing she is fat before this war is coming and making rich and fat like poor and thin. The girl is so shrinking, she is almost like unborn baby—I am knowing because I have been taking them from their mother's belly to be seeing who is girl and who is boy. Are you my mother, I am saying. Are you my sister? But they are only screaming like Devil is coming for them. I am not Devil. I am not bad boy. I am not bad boy. Devil is not blessing me and I am not going to hell. But still I am thinking maybe Devil born me and that is why I am doing all of this.

But I am standing outside myself and I am watching it all happening. I am standing outside of myself. I am grabbing the woman and her daughter. They are not my mother and my sister. I am telling them, it is enough. This is the end.

And now the woman is praying to God, please take my daughter safely to heaven. Forgive her sin. You are saying blessed is the children and who is living in You. They are never seeing death. Am I wronging You? I am trying to live for You. Please Lord I am begging to You. I am laughing laughing because God is forgetting everybody in this country.

Strika is pulling down his short and showing that he is man to this woman while I am holding her one leg and another soldier is holding the other. She is screaming, DEVIL BLESS YOU! DEVIL BORN YOU! But it is not Devil that is borning me. I am having father and mother and I am coming from them.

She is still screaming screaming, AYIIIEEE, like it is the creation of my village when long ago great warrior and his army are just fighting fighting enemy in the bush near my village. They are fighting for many day, but nobody is winning until finally they are growing tired and saying, let us stop. Let us stop. So they are stopping and feasting together, enemy with enemy, and rejoicing well well until they are going to sleep. But in the night enemy is attacking warrior and wounding him until he is running away into the bush. It is at this time that he is falling down by this river and almost dying, but the goddess of the river is coming to help him and make him better. She was the most beautiful thing to be seeing in the whole world so when the warrior is waking up to see her he is saying Kai! and falling in love right there. Then, because he is loosing from his own village he is saying, well I will just marry this beautiful woman so that we can be having some children which is exactly what he is doing at the time. When the woman is having her baby, she is having twin boy, very strong because of their father being warrior and their mother being goddess. Also, because of their mother being goddess, they could be changing from one animal to the other. So sometimes they are changing into monkey to be climbing into the tree and getting the best fruit and sometimes they are changing to bird to be seeing the whole world. And they are loving each other so much until one day they are changing into different animal. One is becoming ox to be going to the river to drink because he is thirsty and the other is becoming leopard so that he can be hunting in the bush. Leopard was hunting hunting, but he is not finding anything to be killing so he is coming back to find his mother and his father. When he is coming to the river, he is seeing this ox just standing there drinking and he is saying, oho I will be killing this thing and bringing food back for my family to be eating. He is coming to Ox very quietly until he is so close he is biting Ox on the neck, but at the same time Ox is fighting him and chooking him in the heart with his two big horn. Since they are wounding, they are changing back into human being and seeing that they are brother and not enemy so they are crying crying until they are dying right there and their blood is just running into the river and turning it to brown. Their mother and their father are coming back and finding them dead just like that and the mother is screaming AYIIIEEE and crying and saying that she is needing to get away from this place where her children are dead because it is abomination. So, they are moving up the hill to where the square of the village is now and having more children, but every year, goddess and warrior are coming back to this river with all of the rest of their children to be visiting the place where their son is dying.

AYIIIEEE! woman is just looking at me and screaming. And I am shouting, SHUTUP! SHUTUP! SHUTUP! This woman is enemy. She is killing my family and burning my house and stealing my food and making my family to scatter. And this girl is enemy. She is killing my father and making me to run from my home. I am pulling the girl, but she is not letting go of her mother's arm. She is holding holding her so the two of them are like one animal. I am with Strika and we are pulling the girl, pulling until her leg is cracking, but she is not letting go. She is screaming and I am seeing her breath is coming out from her mouth, just coming out and coming out. Then Strika is taking his knife high above his head and chopping and everybody is coming apart.

The girl is having no more hand.

She is not screaming or shouting or making any noise. She is just having no more hand. Commandant is saying that she is enemy, she is stealing our food, and killing my family because she is enemy. I am jumping on her chest KPWUD KPWUD and I am jumping on her head, KPWUD, until it is only blood that is coming out of her mouth.

You are not my mother, I am saying to the girl's mother and then I am raising my knife high above my head. I am liking the sound of knife chopping KPWUDA KPWUDA on her head and how the blood is just splashing on my hand and my face and my feets. I am chopping and chopping and chopping until I am looking up and it is dark.

Another night.

Time is passing. Time is not passing. Day is changing to night. Night is changing to day. How can I know what is happening? It is like one day everything is somehow okay even if we are fighting war, but the next day we are killing killing and looting from everybody. How can I know what is happening to me? How can I know?

Everything is inside out like my shirt I am wearing. Sometimes I am seeing thing in front of me when we are walking or drilling or killing, and sometimes I am seeing thing that I am knowing is coming from before the war, but I am seeing it like they are coming right now. If person is dancing or singing in the camp just to be doing something to not be thinking about war, then I am closing my eye and seeing how when I am in my village we are loving so much to dance. We are dancing too because it is how we are learning to become men. Young person is having to spend one whole year learning all the dance that is turning you to man, and if you are not learning, then nobody is thinking that you are man.

If I am seeing celebration in my village it is because I am closing my eye and seeing how everybody is coming to the village square and the men are standing to one side while the womens and childrens and boy who are not dancing are standing on the other. It is starting in the morning when the air is still cool and it is fulling of the smoke from everybody's morning fire. I am remembering how the village square is always being swept clean by all the dancer and how the broom is making line in the sand from the chief's house all the way to the gray wall of the church.

Every year this is happening, my mother is grumbling, it is not good to be celebrating any spirit but God because He is jealous and will be punishing you. But she was still tying her white cloth around her body and wrapping her head in white cloth to be joining the other woman cooking the whole night in the compound of the village chief. And when she is grumbling like this, my father is saying, God is knowing that we are only worshiping Him truly, but there are other spirit that we must also be saying hello to

In the morning, the whole village was standing in the square and wearing their white cloth. I was always looking at all the woman and how they are shutting their eye from tiredness and how the men who are standing are jumping and shaking like they are wanting to be dancing again. Then I am looking to the drummer who are sitting and cracking their finger and putting their ear on the goatskin of their drum just listening to what the drum is wanting to say. And the air was tighting like top of the drum and everybody in the whole place was just agitating.

Everyone is just standing around and agitating when each noise is coming and thinking, is this the time, is this the beginning, but the beginning was never coming when you are thinking. Everybody is just stopping to wait and talking talking about this and that when KPWOM! the first drum is beating and AYI-IIEEE! then first dancer is shouting out to be telling everyone to shutup and just be watching. All the dancer is dancing the Dance of the Warrior and they are coming out wearing bell on their ankle and carrying machete that they are making from wood. All of the mask on the face is painting with color bright like sunrise, color that is dancing almost as much as they are dancing when the drum is beating and the bell is ringing. They are wearing grass hat that is just talking like the wind in the grasses when they are jumping this way and that way pretending to be fighting until dust is flying everywhere and making people to have catarrh too much.

Then all the dancer is disappearing just like that and everybody was sweating and shouting and smiling before we are feasting on yam with red palm oil, and fish, and meat, and egg with pepper that are making the mouth to be feeling fire so you are having to drink so much water. At this time, the women are talking to themself and the men are talking to themself and the children are playing. But me, I am wanting to dance too much so I am trying to be repeating the dance I am seeing.

And before you are even ready, KPWOM! AYIEEE! And all the dancer is coming back to be dancing the Dance of the Goddess in mask of white chalk and blue paint on their body and blue cloth around their waist. No drum is beating this time, but the women of the village are singing loudly loudly the song of the river goddess while the men are watching and moving from one foot to the other foot.

And in the afternoon, we are eating some more pounded yam and soups with goat meat and oxtail, or rice with chicken and plantain, or roasted maize and salad with leaf fresh from the farm, but nobody is really jubilating because the song is so sweet that it is making you to want to cry, and if you are talking then you are disturbing how sweet it is.

When evening was finally coming and the sun is setting so the only light is coming from the torch burning in the village square, we are dancing the Dance of the Ox and Leopard. All the dancer was shining with oil and sweat and their feets stomping the ground and their dress is shaking grasses all over the ground. In the orange light, they are looking like spirit themself just dancing in ox-head mask with sharp horn coloring red and white, and also leopard mask with sharp teeths coloring red and white. I am liking this dance the best, how the ox and leopard are just running at each other and falling back, running and falling back, and snapping their arm and their leg, throwing their head from this side to that side until the end of the dance when so much sweat is running down their arm it is looking like the color of blood in the orange light.

With all of the song from the day sounding in the air above us, the whole village was collecting all our torch, picking up the fire from the square and walking down the road past all of the compound, down to where the path is cutting through palm grove and down to the river. Everybody is rushing rushing because mosquito was biting us and also to be seeing who the head boy cutting the ox will be.

By the river, tied to one palm tree by its horn and its leg an ox was always waiting and stomping and making long low noise that are making you to sadding very much in your heart. The whole village was watching as all the dancer is dancing in the shallow river until the whole water is shining with small small wave. Then the top boy is going to the village chief and kneeling before him while the other leopard and ox dancer are dancing around and around him. The chief is giving him real machete and saying something into his ear until the boy is going and chopping one blow into the neck of the ox. Blood is flying all over his body and he is wiping it from his mask with his hand. Then he is putting his hand where he is cutting and collecting the blood to be rubbing on his body. When he is finishing, all the other is doing the same until everyone is covering in so much blood. They are spinning and spinning in their leopard mask or ox mask until KPWOM! the drum is sounding.

Everybody is knowing that to be killing masquerade you are removing its mask.

All of the dancer is removing their mask.

All of the spirit are dying and now all the boy is becoming men.

I am opening my eye and seeing that I am still in the war, and I am thinking, if war is not coming, then I would be man by now.

If I am closing my eye, I am seeing the rainy season and how, in my village, they are saying it is always bringing change too fast. You can be starting in one place with one plan and then finding that the whole world is washing away beneath your feets. You can be walking on road and finding that you are swimming in river. You can be starting day all dry and warm and then be finishing with your clothe like another skin on your body. Nothing is ever for sure and everything is always changing.

It is not like one day I am going to sleep and the next day I am waking up and there is war, but it still is not like we are having time to prepare for this war because everything was still happening so fast that we were not even knowing what really happened.

One day, they are closing school because there is no more Government. Part of me is feeling sad because I am liking to be in school and learning. Part of me is also happy because sometimes sitting in the hot classroom and just sweating while everybody else is making noise and all of the younger people are crying is making me to angry. Anyway, we are not having anything to be doing so early one morning I am going to Dike's house because I am knowing he was always waking up early. I went to be standing outside waiting for him because his mother is not liking us to disturb her so early in the morning and I am waiting, waiting, waiting, waiting for so long until the sun is full in the sky and the chicken are starting to fighting each other and quarreling over the insect and rubbish in the gutter. I was waiting but no one was coming out.

So I was just standing outside Dike's house just watching and looking at how big and nice his house is. It is having nice paint that is always looking fresh, and window that is always looking washed, and also the compound around the house is looking very fine because someone is always cutting the grasses and his father is making sure that nobody is leaving rubbish inside the compound so there is nothing like chicken or goat coming to be eating and messing up the place. I was always wanting to go inside the house, but I am knowing not to because Dike's mother is not wanting me inside to be messing up the place with my dirty shoe.

But this time I am standing outside of Dike's house, I am not hearing any of the normal sound like music or singing or crying or shouting coming from inside. I am running around trying all of the door and beating on the iron bar of the window with my hand, but they are locking tight which is not normal because someone was always home at his house. This was making my belly to feel big and too small because Dike is my best friend at this time and I am hoping that something bad is not happening to him or his family. So, I am sitting on the verandah and not knowing what to be doing to solve this problem.

As I was just sitting is when the cook for Dike's house is coming out from the boys' quarter in the back and asking me what I am doing this morning and why I am sitting on the verandah if this is not my house. If you had been looking at my face, you would have been seeing so much happiness because I am now believing that nothing is wrong and maybe they are just going somewhere and will be coming back later. I was looking up because of the voice of the cook, but he was looking sad even though he was smiling because his eye is having red color and bending down at the edge like he is crying too much. His clothe are having many wrinkle and stain on them like he is fighting food instead of cooking it and also his hand which he is putting on my head are smelling so much of chicken and other nice meats.

He was telling me that Dike and his mother are leaving the last night to meet his father where they are staying in far-away town. I was just looking. Sometimes when you are hearing what you do not want to be hearing then everything in your body stops to working and all you can be doing is looking because unless you are blind then your eye never stop looking. That is how I am looking because my mouth is not working enough for me to speak and even my leg are hardly working for me to move.

Papa said they should just be leaving before war is coming to mess this place up, he is saying to me and I am just looking, but in my head I was feeling so angry because Dike was not telling me if he was leaving. And at all time, we are telling each other all thing because we are best friend almost like brother. So now I was sitting not knowing what to be doing with my day as there was no school and no Dike. I was feeling like somebody is coming to take everything that I like and just make me to sad. And I am watching the cook, who even though he was still smiling, was also looking sad because he was complaining. Even since I go cook them this food, for all this time. Madam can't even leave nothing for me to find my own way home. Because I no have money like Madam does it mean I no have family to go for find, he was saying to me.

He was sitting next to me and stretching his leg out in front of us so that I am seeing his leg and how they are full of mosquito bite and other dark spot. It was making me to feel somehow in my head and belly when I am looking at it.

I am saying, sorry sorry oh, but he was not even listening to me because he is too busy talking to himself.

Devil bless Madam. Only bad thing go happen to her from now on, he was saying and shaking all the fly away from his head and feets.

Then because I was still feeling angry in my head, and because the cook is acting like madman, I was thinking to be going home. And as I am walking on the road that is going to my home, I am seeing only the feets of all the other people who were living in or had come back to the village because my anger was weighing my head forward. So because of this I am not greeting the older people as I should be doing, but nobody was saying anything to me because they were all having their own worry and I was just going on my way until the old woman who is always sitting on her chair selling groundnut that nobody is buying because person are fearing that she is some sort of witch was saying, you are not wanting to greet me? These young person not behaving well anymore, just acting like animal. But it is okay. Trouble go follow you.

And I am remembering that woman even now because I am thinking what she is saying is why my life is so bad.

Behind my eye I am seeing how one day, the younger children began to be growing thinner. Their belly are becoming rounder because other part of their body was growing smaller.

When they are running around in the village they are having to hold their clothe to their body because even the elastic was not tighting their trouser enough. My sister was looking this way with her neck and her arm and leg becoming less strong. She was becoming slower in everything she was doing. When she was washing the plate, her head was tipping to her chest and her arm was becoming harder for her to move so that too much water would be splashing in every different direction and causing my mother to scream. But really, even though she was screaming on us all the time, I am knowing inside my head, also because I am hearing her praying, that she is fearing and feeling sad that we are so thin.

Then the people started coming back and everything was changing. The first one that were coming are looking okay. You could see from how their eye is looking this way and that they are fearing, like they are waiting for some animal to jump out from the bush. But when they were coming, they are coming in their car which were filling with more of thing they are owning than with people. Electrician is coming with their electrical thing, Tailor with all of their clothe. Banker with all of his money.

And when they started coming on transport and bus, there were so many women and their children, so many new people that every day everyone from the village is getting dressed very early to go and be waiting at the bus stop and car park to be watching for which relative is returning home and also to be praying that everyone is returning safely.

And then they are taking the light, but it is not changing how we are living too much. My mother is never using electricity to cook and my father's radio is using battery, so we are living like normal. My father was still going into town because his school is still meeting, but then one day, my mother is waking to find me and my father sitting together and looking at how the iron he is heating in the fire is just burning his shirt. The spot was just looking brown and crinkly, making the shirt to look like toilet paper. My father was looking to cry and biting his lip. He is wiping sweat from his forehead with the back of his hand and using his rappa to be cleaning his finger.

They are telling me not to be coming anymore. There is no more school, he is saying through his shirt he is holding up to his mouth. I am wanting to cry for him because I am knowing that he is never crying himself. I am wanting to open my mouth and scream so that everybody is waking up and listening to all of the trouble this war is bringing, but my mother and my father are keeping quiet so I am keeping quiet also.

My mother was just standing facing the compound. Her own clothe was wrapped under her armpit just where the hairs is sticking together from the sweat of her sleep. She is not turning around to us, but she is not stepping away or even holding the iron bar on the verandah to be helping her stand up. My father is touching his beard and asking what are we going to do and then he is just looking at my mother's back.

She is saying, stop looking at me and start praying. God is always helping you if you are asking Him. Then she is walking to the kitchen and leaving me and my father just sitting and staring at all the plant in the compound. My father is putting his head in his shirt and saying nothing. I am confusing. How can my father just be sitting there looking like goat that is ready to die? I was getting up to get water for my bath and leaving my father there for the whole day. He was just sitting and not even saying one word to anyone, not even to my sister who is always making him to laugh and be talking talking. I am not knowing if he is going to bed that night because he was still sitting there when I am coming to lock the gate and hang the key.

And then one day, when I am sweeping the parlor, just bending over and using broom to get all of the dust from each corner of the room, my father is rushing into the room sweating like he was running very fast. I am seeing how the sweat is just soaking through his shirt and making his face to shine and I am standing there looking at him wondering what is happening that is making him to look like this. My father is shouting to me, get up! Come on, we are having to go to the church NOW! And I am wondering what it is that is happening because it is not even Sunday. I am wanting to go and change into something, but my father is saying to move quick quick and to get my mother so we can be going to church. I am moving quickly and running out to the kitchen where my mother was just humming over one pot of stew, but when she is seeing me, right away she is thinking that something is wrong and so she is running to meet my father on the verandah where he is waiting. And then they are shouting and I am hearing my mother saying, heyeye! The war is come oh! War is coming.

I am asking if I can be going with them to the church and they are saying yes, so my father is carrying my sister who is sleeping because she is having nothing better to do and I am walking with my mother up the path of my village to the church. Even before we are getting inside, I am hearing voice that are even too loud to be coming from service. People are shouting and talking too loud and I am not even able to hear one sentence that anybody is speaking. When we are getting inside the church, the whole place was too hot and smelling like animal because there is no electricity and all the fan cannot be moving round and round to be bringing some air. Everybody in the village was trying to fit into the church so some people are standing on the bench, and other people are leaning on the wall, and everybody is just sweating because it is like we are one million cow just being put in the same space to be living. I am seeing so many people—even people who are not coming to this church, just talking talking and shouting shouting like something bad is going to happen. Pastor and the Chief are standing at the front of the church and shouting, but because there is no microphone nobody was really hearing them and everybody was talking over their talking. Pastor is just getting angry and running to one big drum set that is there and beating the symbol well well until the whole place is sounding KWANG! KWANG! KWANG! We are all shutting up. We are all shutting up except for the sound of too many people breathing.

Pastor was not even wearing his white robe when he is walking around at the front of the church. Instead, he was just wearing one blue shirt and trouser and also one cap to be covering his bald head. He was shouting shouting, DO YOU HEAR! WE CANNOT JUST BE SITTING HERE LIKE COW UNTIL THEY ARE BRINGING THE WAR! It is saying in The Bible that God is only helping those who are helping themselves. Isn't God protecting the Israelites when they are having to leave their own home? So let us be pleasing God and leaving until the fighting is no more in our area. Otherwise they will just be killing killing all of us and then what will we be doing? I am laughing in my head even though my heart is beating fast fast with all of this talk of killing because I am thinking how my father is saying that Pastor is thinking he can be talking so much because he is having his Reverend Doctorate that is making him doctor of talking.

Then the Chief was getting up and wearing his red cap and his black shirt and saying, yes. Yes Pastor is right. We should be leaving. They are telling me that UN is coming to help us go, so when they are coming, we will be going with them. Tomorrow, at least all of the women and the small small children will be going with them first and then after we are making sure that everything is okay with all of the thing we are owning then the men can be finding their way to safety. Am I making it clear?

And then there was shouting shouting, WHO IS UN? WHAT ABOUT MY FARM? AND MY GOAT? AND WHAT ABOUT ALL MY BOOK? OR MY CAR? ENH! WHAT ABOUT ALL OF THESE THING! The voice are just coming from all of the different place in the church and every time somebody is shouting one thing then every head is turning to that direction to be seeing what it is they are shouting. There was too much grumbling and it was making my head to hurt so I am just standing near to my mother and my father and trying to be making sure that I am not annoying anybody. When we are finishing, everybody is leaving the church and nobody is even remembering to say a prayer because everybody is fearing how the fighting is coming too too near. I am not hearing anything, but my father who is already surviving one war is saying that you will know when war is coming if you are seeing airplane and hearing GBWEM GBWEM which is meaning that they are shelling and bombing.

That night my mother is making a big dinner of all my favorite food which is rice and stew with so much meats, but nobody, not even my father who can be eating three whole plate and even going back for more, is able to be eating anything at all at all. After dinner, I am clearing the table and stacking all the plate in one corner because it is even too dark to be washing and when I am coming back to the house I am seeing my mother like one dark spot and the light from the lamp was all around her while she was just packing food into many small bag. I was going to her and tapping her on her elbow to be asking, where we are going to go? And she is saying to me, we are going where we will be going and we will be getting there when we are getting there. I am not even knowing what she is meaning when she is saying this kind of thing, but then I am asking her if she is fearing, and she is looking back at me and bringing me close and hugging me so that my head is resting in her breast. Why should I be fearing Agu? Enh, she is saying. Aren't you remembering that the Lord is protecting everybody and making sure that nothing bad will ever be happening to us? Now go and get ready for bed okay. And don't be forgetting to pray. No matter what is happening remember that God is only remembering those who are praying.

So I am running through the hallway and into the room I am sharing with my sister and when I am getting there I am seeing that she is putting one knife under her bed. What is this for, I am asking her while I am looking at it with lamp and she is saying, for the enemy if they are coming, and then turning her head to be facing the wall. And I am laughing small small even if I am fearing because sometimes my sister, even though she is young, is trying to be too smart.

I was lying down to be sleeping in my own bed, but my whole body was just feeling so hot and everywhere was itching too much like ant is biting me. I am trying to sleep, trying to sleep, but I was not even closing my eye. It was like I am waiting for Father Christmas, and I am just lying there until the middle of the night when I am hearing my mother and my father talking. What do you mean you are not coming, my mother is saying to my father and I am hearing my father saying back, how can Agu be coming with you if we are supposed to be the men of this village? What is that looking like if everybody is staying to make sure their house is all right and we are just running from place to place? Enh? That is not right. And my mother is saying back to him, no. No. Just remove that thought from your head. God forbid such thing enh. And my father is saying, you are not understanding anything here. And my mother is saying, what if you are going and dying, then what am I doing? Do you want me to be sitting by the roadside like some woman with no sense who is just pulling out her hairs and trying to sell it? Then my father is just shouting, Wait now! It is my duty and it is his duty as my first son to be—before my mother is shouting,

YOUR SON THIS AND THAT! Sometimes I am thinking that
you are having no sense at all. Let me just be taking him with me
enh. If there is war and everybody is dying, then who is even
going to say anything if he is not staying around?

My belly was starting to tight too much because I am lying
and thinking that I am not wanting to be seeing all the killing,
but I am also knowing that I cannot just be leaving my father
alone here and running off otherwise all of the other men will
be laughing at him. So I am just staring at the roof and listening
to the rainwater going PAH PAH PAH on the roof and to the
lizard that is trying to find place to hide from the heavy rain, but
I am not sleeping because I am fearing too too much.

The next morning my father is waking me, but I am so so
tired and his face was just looking too tired also. He was moving
around too fast and just agitating everywhere. I am asking him,
where are we going and he is saying, don't worry. Don't worry.

Later, we are all walking to the center of the village with my
mother and sister just carrying this small load and that small load
that they are taking with them. So many person was standing
there that it is looking like how it is looking during the festival,
only nobody is smiling at all. Each family was just staying in one
corner and you are seeing all of the mother with their small
small children just sitting next to one red-and-white-striped bag
that was holding everything they can be taking at one time. And
we were just waiting, waiting until the rain is starting to fall onto
everything and sticking to it like million tiny insect. Everybody
was trying to get into one building or another building in the

village square to be waiting and everybody was just looking sad. The men are looking tired and the women are fearing. It is only the small small children that are not knowing what is happening.

Late in the afternoon we are hearing all of many truck rumbling up, big white truck with the letter UN in black on the side. Soldier in blue helmet and green camouflage is just jumping down from the truck even as they are moving and their tire is just chewing up the whole ground. They are shouting to just remain in order, and then they are shouting at us to load up onto all the truck and I am looking at my father who is helping my mother to be carrying one bag to the truck with all of the other women and their children. I am seeing how my father's mouth is just being pulled down at the edge, and I am seeing how he is not even wanting to be letting go of my sister or my mother. My mother is touching me and holding me and telling me to remember to be praying praying all the time and not to be worrying, that we will be seeing each other soon. I am seeing my father pushing my mother onto the truck and then I am remembering how her hand is feeling in my own hand and then I am remembering standing with my father while she and my sister are just going away on the truck and that is the last time I am ever seeing them.

And I am seeing behind my eye how it is just men and boy in the village sadding too much because war is taking everything away from us. Nothing in the village is the same without women cooking food and selling groundnut and talking talking so all of the men are just staying quietly quietly like somebody is dying. I am seeing all of this and I am seeing how one day, I was not seeing excepting light that was pushing through hole in the roof, but it was not enough. The whole place was so hot and I am sweating too much. My short was soaking through and my shirt was touching my body like skin. How many of us are there just sitting in this place? I am not knowing, but I am thinking maybe ten or fifteen or even more. There are too many that our fear is just smelling and the whole room is just tasting like salt. Outside I am hearing bullet everywhere and shouting and screaming.

I am asking my father, will they be killing us? Will they be killing us?

Somebody was slapping my face and saying SHUTUP. Is it my father who was slapping me? It is so dark, but I am knowing it is not him. My mouth was filling with blood and I am knowing the color of blood is red just red everywhere. I was wiping my mouth with my arm, but my sweat was making my lip to sting too much. I was wanting to see, but the only light that was here is coming through small small hole in the ceiling. The door was locked and I am trapped. We are all trapped because of the bullet outside.

I am hearing my father's voice, look. You can be dying now or dying later. It is all the same. Are you wanting to sit here until they are coming to burn us to ash? Enh? Remember now, you can only be dying once. If you are not dying standing anyway, you will be walking on your knee with all the ancestor. I am knowing that this is bad thing because if you are walking on your knee, then you are always having to look up when somebody is talking to you, and if they are talking to you, then their spits will just be flying into your face. A voice is saying, I am rather to be living now inside than to just be dying like animal outside. And people are whispering, yes, yes. And my father is whispering, then your son will be spitting on your grave enh.

And more people are whispering, yes yes. It is true. It is true. Are we ready?

Nobody is saying anything at all, but I am hearing machete scraping the floor. Outside it is still sounding of bullet and laughing like goat chewing on metal. I am fearing so much that my feets is feeling like they are belonging to the man standing next to me. And my hand is feeling like they are being carved from stone. My father was telling me that when we are going out I should just be running running. Running in the other direction. It is okay, he is saying. It is okay. If you are running fast, then the enemy won't be seeing you. I am asking to him if we are going to die, but he is not saying anything. It is all quiet except for everybody breathing like cow or goat in the pen. Will we die, I am asking? Will they be killing us? I am having another slap on my face.

Bullet was just sounding so loud and there was so much screaming and shouting and laughing. They are finding us. Somebody was groaning and mumbling that they will be using our body after they are killing us. They will just be loading us onto one truck, bleeding like that so our blood is dripping from the edge and flying off into the wind. And they will be driving us into the bush so we cannot even be buried in our own village and just leaving us for the animal to be eating like that. Another person is saying that they will be playing with our body and using our intestine as whip to be whipping each other and cutting off our hand and holding them to be shaking each other. One more voice was saying, they are the Devil, I am seeing it with my own eye. They are looking like monster with half face, long fingernail, and sharp teeths. He is saying they are looking like the Devil because you cannot even be living long enough to see them, and if you are living, then you are already becoming Devil like them.

Shutup! Shutup! There is no time, somebody is shouting and then I am hearing another person counting, one, two, three and the door is opening to let in so much light that is blinding me. I am not seeing anything anymore, just white light everywhere. I am hearing everybody sucking in breath and I am sucking in breath too. The air is smelling of burning wood and gunpowder and gasoline. I am hearing more shouting and then I am hearing my father saying run. RUN! RUN! AGU RUN! and I am saying, I am running if the other man is not having my leg, but then somebody is pushing me and I am just running. I am seeing soldier with black face and big white smile. I am seeing bullet making my father to dance everywhere with his arm raising high to the sky like he is praising God. I am hearing terrible laughing and I am running, running, running through the mud, but the mud is trying to hold me. I am smelling how it is smelling like the butcher shop and I am hearing, THEY ARE KILLING ME OH! JESUS CHRIST HELP ME! HELP ME! I am seeing man running with no head like chicken, and I am seeing arm and leg everywhere. Then everything is just white and all I am hearing is step slap, step slap, step slap, and the sound of my own breathing.

All of this is really happening to me? It is all happening like it is happening again and I cannot even be believing it.

I am opening my eye and seeing how everywhere is dark in some place and orange with fire and lamp in other place. I am seeing men lying everywhere with gun lying next to them. My heart is beating beating, so fast. I am feeling thirsty.

We are at the camp and I am watching how the sun is just dropping down behind the hill like it is not wanting to be seeing us anymore. All the color is leaking out of it and looking like flame from hell all over, eating up the top of all the tree, making all the leaf bright, bright. Suddenly it is night. The earth is changing from bright orange to black and I am seeing steam rising up from some darkness, just chasing the sun away.

At this time, I am thinking all the building of this camp we are living in is not just the terrible place that we are to be sleeping but are looking almost like simple village house made of palm wood and thatch. I am looking and thinking that if we are not having war, then this place would be too nice to be looking at. All the palm tree, so kind to us, giving us oil and wine, is stretching high up to where they are brushing the sky clear of cloud after it is raining. And when the night is coming, I am thinking the bird and animal should just be singing back and forward to each other before they are going to be sleeping.

But we are coming here and bringing the war. When we are

coming here, we are stripping all the palm tree to build our shelter and because there is no more place to rest all the bird is flying away. The night is now too quiet because we are so hungry that we are eating everything that is making noise. And those thing that we are not catching stopped to making noise so they are not getting eaten. Behind this camp, there is also stream that was just shining in the clear sunshine and smelling so fresh with life that you are even seeing how the fishes is enjoying and the frog and their baby is acting like they are in heaven, but we are emptying our rubbish and using this place for washing ourself and going to toilet so it is becoming terrible to look at.

I am just watching as they are unloading all the thing that we are looting from different village off all the truck. I am watching as the sun is leaving small by small from the sky and how all the color is making truck driver's skin to be shining when they are going into the engine to make sure that they are running well well for the next day. And in the small small light, they are coming out just shining with oil even if it is getting dark. Still if I am looking too hard they are beginning to disappear like ghost. All I am seeing is their eye blinking like all the firefly that are one time living in this area. They are walking to the stream to wash off and their singing is making me to feel somehow at ease. I am stretching my leg out in front of me and placing my hand behind my head.

Every night they are making fire and soldier is sitting down and talking. After some time I am getting up to go and sit with them around the fire. It is warm and it is making me to feel a little bit okay and I am happying to be back at the camp because it is nice here—at least nicer than having to be in place with all of its screaming people that you are killing all the time. And here, I am relaxing because there is no enemy that I have to be watching out for if they are wanting to kill me. But I am sitting here listening to the other men talking and breathing and breathing and somehow looking alive. When it is so, we are really all just waiting to die, I am still sadding too much. I am not liking to be sad because being sad is what happens to you before you are becoming mad. And if you are becoming mad, then it is meaning that you are not going to be fighting. So I cannot be sad because if I cannot be fighting, then either I will die, or Commandant will be killing me. If I am dead, then I will not be able to be finding my mother and my sister when this war is finishing. I am thinking to myself of all the thing that I will do when the war is over and I am alive. And I am thinking that when it is over, I can be going to university to study. I think I am wanting to be Engineer because I like how mechanic is always doing thing to the truck and I like to be watching even though there is no chance for me to try what they are doing. And sometimes I am thinking that I want to be Doctor because then I will be able to be helping people instead of killing them and then maybe I will be forgiven for all my sin. I am thinking that if I am both Doctor or Engineer, these people are the one who are the big men. I know because the richest man in our village—even though he was old and died before the war is coming—he was Doctor and he was always having little monies to be giving out to people who are asking him. He was also big man with fat stomach because he was having lots of monies to be eating a lot of thing here and there. So also when I am big man, I know that I can be reading my book without anyone troubling me like they used to be troubling me before and nobody will be able to say anything to me. I will be saying all the thing to person, telling them to do this and do that and making sure that they bow their head and only look at the ground when they come to greet me, also making sure that they bring me my water when I want it or that they are bringing me my food when I want it. And I will be fat because big men are always fat; they are always having so much to eat. And I will be eating all the food until my stomach is full and then I will be eating even more until my stomach is so full that I will not be able to see my feets even if I am stretching my neck all the way forward. I think that this will be fine because if I am ever not able to eat for long period of time, then at least I will not be turning into ghost like we are turning into because of war.

Then I will go back to church. I will go back to church to ask God for forgiveness every day. And I will go back to church and sit on the bench under the fan that one day will just be falling and crushing me and I will not even be minding the splinter that is chooking into my leg because I will be paying attention to Jesus. I won't even be moving my eye from the statue of Jesus and instead I will just be sitting there watching Him and watching Him until one day He will be telling me that it is okay.

I am smelling food that they are cooking that is making me so hungry. What should I do? When we are killing people, their blood is getting all over the food we are stealing from them. It is getting all over their animal and vegetable. We are finding farmer and his goat on the road and we are killing him. Now I am not knowing what is farmer and what is goat. And the yam, they are having blood on them. And the rice, they are having blood on them. All the other soldier are saying that since they are boiling it that nothing will be happening to us, but I am not thinking you can be boiling away the blood of farmer even if you are boiling rice or yam forever. But I am hungry and I am eating vegetable and fruit and rice and meats and I am not thinking anymore. I am only eating. When we are eating, we are not speaking. We are so hungry and just eating and eating until we are so full all we can be doing is sleeping sleeping.

We are going to be sleeping in our four building that we are making them of stick and palm thatch. They are not even having any wall, just roof to keep the rain from beating us, so all of the insect is coming up to us in the night. There is not enough room for all of us under these building, so some soldier is sleeping outside where the rain can be falling on them. No animal is coming up to eat anybody because they are all gone away. They are so afraid of us that they are not wanting to come back.

We are all lying down to sleep, but I am not sleeping. I cannot be sleeping. I can never be sleeping. I am just listening listening. No noise. Then I am hearing one boy talking talking. We are calling him Griot because he is always telling story when we are falling asleep. This is story he is telling:

I was just with my mother when the war is coming, he is saying. This is how he is starting every night when we are trying to be sleeping. We are just in the market to get some food because we are having no food to eat, not even the skin of cassava. I was just in the market when I am hearing GBWEM! I am just hearing one blast and the whole ground began to shaking shaking. And then those government pilot, they are just coming in low with their screaming plane and I was covering my ear, but the drum were just beating BOTU BOTU BOTU because the pilot was shooting TAKA TAKA TAKA and everybody is running this way and that way. This one is hiding under wheelbarrow. That one is hiding in church. This one is jumping in gutter. I am not knowing where to be hiding so I am just running running up and down the road. I am hearing another GBWEM landing right next to me. And then I was feeling fire on my body but I wasn't burning. When I am looking up, I am seeing people hanging from tree like piece of meat. Head just hanging like coconut before it is falling off. Ah ah. Nah wah oh!

No noise.

But not for too long because he is starting again. He is saying, my mother. My mother. Heyeye now. My mother is dead. All of her meats just hanging from tree. Then he is coughing and beginning to shake—I am hearing him moving on the ground where he is lying.

And then there is boy we are calling Preacher who is not coming from village. He is coming from the bush. He is twisting around in his sleeping and singing song I am never hearing before. Thou art worthy. Thou art worthy oh Lord, he is singing in his deep voice that is making me to fear because it is sounding like it is coming from nowhere, from spirit. Preacher is having Bible that he is using as pillow sometimes. That is why we are calling him Preacher. His Bible is so tattered that it is not even staying together by itself anymore and he is having to hold it together with piece of old shirt. He is keeping it in his pocket with his knife and his extra bullet.

But he is asleep and singing, thou art worthy. Thou art worthy oh Lord, over and over again. I am not asleep, and I am now singing with him even if I am not knowing all the word. For thou has created. All thing and for thy pleasure. They a-a-are and were created. Thou art worthy, because the song keeps going round and round and round again and again.

But then there is light shining in my face and when I am opening my eye it is blinding me. I am stopping to breathing because I am seeing Strika's face looking like spirit or demon. His skin is looking somehow like burned-up wood or charcoal and it is sticking tight to his face so his whole cheek is sticking out sharp sharp. I am saying, leave me. Leave me alone. But then I am looking in his eye and the way that he is trying to tell me that I should not be lying here and that I should be hurrying up—Commandant is wanting to see me right now. I am not liking it when Commandant is wanting to see me, but I am having to go otherwise it will be making him to angry. I am getting up, but it is not easy to do this. And when I am standing up I am stretching my body and watching as Strika is going back quickly to his own place where he is sleeping which is under one of the truck with all of the truck driver. Then I am picking up my knife that I am having with me because I am never leaving my knife just in case the enemy is coming and I am stepping over people's head and feets to be getting to where Commandant is staying. The way I am walking through the darkness, I am like animal in the night. Tonight it is all so quiet and I am thinking it is because of the killing we are doing. I am walking this way and just stepping over people and stepping around them and their gun and knife trying not to be waking them up so that there will not be any kind of trouble.

Then I am walking past the other soldier to Commandant's own quarter and just watching him through his mosquito net as he is moving back and forwards. He is the only one with mosquito net. I am seeing the shadow that he is making as he is moving around his room and I am thinking that only big man can be making such big shadow.

When I am reaching the shack, I am looking through the net and seeing Commandant. They are calling him the man who is driving the enemy to madness. He is fighting in many battle even if he is only young man, so he is always telling story of people who are treating death like lover and child who can kill before they can even speak. And he is always saying that he is seeing thing that are making even the Devil fall to his knee and be begging for mercy. He is always saying that he is eating people, but it is not tasting too good. And he is saying he is seeing people eat people like they are real meats.

I am waiting outside in the darkness making myself ready for when I go in. So I am thinking as many good thing I can think because if you are thinking good thing, nothing bad is happening to you.

Each time I am going to Commandant, I am feeling that I should not go in because I am knowing what he is wanting to do to me. I am thinking that each time I should be telling him that I do not want to fight anymore and that he should let me go and become refugee so that at least I will not be having to kill people. But I know that if I am saying this to him, he will be doing the same thing he is doing when he is not happy which is smiling and licking his teeths with his tongue. Then he will just laugh, but it will be angry laugh that he is doing when he is thinking somebody is becoming spy.

Commandant is sitting on the floor with all of his map lying next to him. Even though I am standing at the doorway for long time, he is not looking up at me. I am coughing to be letting him know that I am here, but he is still not looking at me and instead he is looking so tired, just like the rest of us because he is not wearing his dress uniform. He is having only one rappa tied around his waist and between his leg and dirty shirt on. And he is kneeling down on the ground wiping sweat from his head with that same dirty white handkerchief that I am always seeing him using for everything he is doing. It is even looking like he is talking to himself because of all of the thing that he is trying to look at though the light is not bright enough for me to even be seeing my hand if I am holding them up in front of me. When he is on the ground, he is not looking so good because he is having all his finger in his mouth and is rubbing the top of his bald head with the other hand.

What is taking you so long, he is saying to me before I am coming in. Then he is saying, sit down, pointing to cot in the corner of the room. He is Commandant so he is always getting cot to sleep on while the rest of us is sleeping on whatever there is to be sleeping on—if you are lucky it is mat, but mostly it is the ground. Even so, it is not changing anything of what I am thinking while I am standing at the door because I am not liking at all at all how his room is smelling—like animal house after animal is passing the food he is eating—or how this smell is making my nostril to sting like I am breathing in something very sharp like metal. I am also not wanting to move because I am fearing that I am in trouble even if I am not doing anything wrong today. I am moving myself slowly slowly around the edge of the hut, feeling the branch of the thatch chooking into my buttom as I am sliding along to the cot. By the time I am reaching the cot and sitting down, he is still looking at the map and taking Biro to be drawing out thing even if it is so dark he is hardly seeing. I am also thinking as I am rubbing the mud off my feets and then folding my arm up in my lap how it is strange that all of these men are always looking at this whole country on map and acting as if it is piece of meat they can just be dividing by cutting it with knife.

Commandant is just coughing and rubbing his head and arm and talking to himself before finally he is blowing out the candle one by one by one until all the room is dark. When he is finished, I am looking through the mosquito net to where I can see the fire outside. It is very low now, but still I am wanting to be outside where the other soldier is sleeping, where Griot is talking and Preacher is singing, but I am not saying this to Commandant. He is telling me, take off your clothe.

I do not want to be taking off my clothe, but I am not saying so because Commandant is powerful more than me and he is also sometimes giving me small small favor like more food or protection and other thing like shirt or trouser for doing this thing with him. It is making me to feel a bit better when he is giving me these thing because I am knowing that he can be doing what he is wanting to do with me and not giving me anything after. I am hearing him walk over to me where I am sitting on the cot. He is taking off my clothe for me and then he is sitting down next to me and breathing hard, but not like he is running very hard and trying to catch his breath, a different breathing in my ear that I am not liking to listen to at all at all. Then he is beginning to touch me all over with his finger while he is breathing just even harder. But each time he is doing this to me, he is telling me, it is what commanding officer is supposed to be doing to his troop. Good soldier is following order anyway and it is order for you to let me touch you like this. I don't want to be good soldier but I am not saying that. I don't want to be soldier at all. I don't want his finger creeping all over my body. I don't want his tongue to be touching me and feeling like slug should be feeling if it is on your body. I don't want it on my back and even on my leg. And I am thinking it is not good for Commandant to be doing this to me. But I am not saying any of this. I am not saying anything at all. It is making me to angry and it is making me to sad, the thing that he is doing to me. I am knowing that I am not the only one he is doing this to and that is not making me to happy.

Commandant is touching me and bringing my head to where he is standing at attention. As he is doing it, and I am smelling his smell and feeling how much it is making me to want to vomit, I am thinking about the very first time he is doing this and yelling to me, touch his soldier. It is seeming like so long long ago, but this is not mattering because each time it is still feeling like the very first time. This first time I am even lucky because we are not in place like this and there is bed that is not cot. But even so, that time he was telling me to kneel down on the floor and then he is removing his belt and I am fearing so much that I am doing something wrong and that he is going to beat me so hard for what I am doing even if I am not knowing what it is. That time he was saying, relax. I am not punishing you. Then he is saying, remove your clothe.

So I was removing them. And then, after making me be touching his soldier and all of that thing with my hand and with my tongue and lip, he was telling me to kneel and then he was entering inside of me the way the man goat is sometimes mistaking other man goat for woman goat and going inside of them. If you are watching it, then you are knowing it is not natural thing. But me, I was not struggling because I am knowing that he will be killing me if I am struggling and since I am not wanting to die, I just let him to be moving back and forward even though it is hurting me so so much. That first time because we are still having food and thing, he was putting palm oil all over me to make everything easier, he is saying, so it will not be paining me so much. Sometimes if palm oil is not enough, my buttom is burning like it has fire in it.

That first time after he is finishing and I am leaving him, I was going to lie down, but I could not. I was asking Strika whether his own was hurting so much the first time, and he was drawing me picture in the mud of man bending down with his hand on the ground and gun and bullet shooting up his buttom.

The picture was very funny but I am not smiling. I was feeling I can never be smiling again. I was deciding that it was time for me to leave because I felt that I was bleeding and I did not want to be bleeding in front of him or the other soldier otherwise they might be laughing at me and calling me woman. So, that time I am leaving him in the darkness of the room where we are sleeping and taking the lantern and going on my way to find the stream. This time I am not even fearing because I am so angry and confusing in my head about what was happening that I am just walking along the path not even thinking that there is any animal or spirit or the Devil to come and get me. And when I am reaching the stream, I am letting myself to fall in backward with my buttom first, and then I am feeling the water rising up to my chest and all around my face. If I was brave boy, then I would have been swallowing water or rock or something that would have made me to stop breathing and sink right to the bottom where I would just be staying forever, but I am not wanting to die this way because the ancestor will not be letting you to come and live with them. Instead your spirit will just be living wherever you are leaving your body. I was staying under and holding my breath and then trying to open my mouth, but each time I was becoming afraid and swinging my arm and scaring the frog to be making too much noise.

That first time, I am walking back to my camp in the darkness with all the ancestor making noise in my head, with my feets going this way and that into the thorn because it was hurting me too much to walk straight. I was tripping and pounding and trying to keep the lamp from falling unless Commandant would beat me because the lamp is very costly. It is taking me so long to be getting back to the building where Strika was sleeping that by the time I am returning, I am finding Strika sleeping on his mat. I was not knowing where my own mat was, so I just started lying down on the concrete beside him. Then I was feeling his arm around me even though he is not opening his eye to be showing that he is awake. I was not sleeping and was watching him the whole night, shifting, sucking his finger, grabbing his thing, and beating the air with his hand. When the morning was just coming around, I began to be feeling tired and sleepy even more than I was feeling the pain in my buttom and also in my head, so I slept. I must have been sleeping for long time because when I am waking, Strika was gone, leaving only scratching in the ground next to me saying, God will punish him.

But now he is doing the same to me over and over and over and I am used to it somehow even though it is also making me to feel as if I am still feeling it for the first time. He likes to be whispering to me as if I am woman and this time when he is finishing, he is running his hand up and down my back to wipe away the sweat, and then he is rubbing my head like I am still little boy. He is quieting when we are finishing, so quiet I can hear him cleaning himself with his handkerchief and then sitting back down on the cot.

When he is finishing this time, the light from the fire is still showing through the mosquito net and Commandant is sitting at the edge of the bed with his hand between his leg. He is rocking back and forwards and I am trying to know what he is thinking. I am holding my own hand against my buttom and pressing it to stop the pain. And I am putting my head down in his pillow which is smelling of sweat and having little splinter of chewing stick sticking out from inside it. This his cot is not even strong enough to be holding both of us and is creaking with every breath he is taking. My tongue is shifting back into my mouth because I am afraid that I will be biting it off to stop the pain. He is taking deep breath and sucking in all of the shadow in the room like they are food to him.

Agu, he is saying. But he is so tired his word is dragging instead of jumping off of his tongue. Do you want to know something? Let me tell you something.

I am not wanting to know anything he is telling me. I am not wanting to be hearing his voice even if it is only sounding like dull knife because he is so tired. I am not wanting to hear him breathing or to be smelling the anger or worry in his breath. All of this is making me to want to take the fire from outside and be swallowing it so that it is burning out my inside and making me empty shell. But I am saying Sah! Yes Sah! He is putting his hand on the back of my head and I am swallowing hard. The spit is growing in my mouth and I am drooling on the pillow. He is looking at my back, and I am feeling his eye all up and down my naked body. I can feel his stare crawling on my skin like many ant that is moving slowly slowly on the land and eating the world to many piece in one million tiny bite. I am turning and looking at him from the corner of my eye. Even though the room is not having too much light, I am seeing his eye with the red and it is making me to think he is demon. The light is making his nose to sharp more and his lip to shine too much with saliva from his tongue so he is just looking like he is eating very good meal.

Agu. I am not bad man, he is saying softly and putting his hand on my back.

My tear begin to running down my face and are mixing with my spit in the pillow. I want to be telling him that I cannot be fighting anymore, that my mind is becoming rotten like the inside of fruit. But I am knowing that if I am saying anything like this, he will be slapping me the way he is always slapping all the other soldier—until their bloody teeths is cutting his hand. I am biting into the pillow so I will not be making any noise. I am feeling the wooden splinter digging into the top of my mouth and tongue. I am wanting to leave.

Commandant is dragging his finger down the back of my neck and letting them dance and drum on the bump of my back. They are feeling like many drop of hot hot boiling water. Then he is closing his hand around my own hand and moving them away from my buttom.

Don't worry, he is saying. It will be okay.

We are leaving this place and before we are leaving we are tearing it all down. Tearing it all down. The morning is cool and it feels nice on my skin. And if there is no war and we are normal person and not soldier, we are jubilating and saying, how nice the morning feels. How nice it is before the sun is coming out from all the cloud. We are all waking up and walking around stretching our arm and leg, and we are all hungry. Nobody is eating. Everyone here is doing zero zero one. I am not knowing what this is meaning before I am soldier, but now I am knowing that it means no breakfast, no lunch, only dinner. If you are wanting to eat when it is not dinner, then you are having to keep your dinner from before to be eating the next day. Or if we raiding or finding farm, then we can be eating.

We are all knowing what to do when it is time to be leaving. Food is going in one truck. Kerosene and fuel is going in another truck, and everybody is making sure he is having his own gun or knife because if you are losing this gun or knife, then Commandant will be losing you.

So this is what we are doing, loading this and loading that until finally we are pulling all of the building into one pile of palm and wood and so before we are leaving the camp, we can be burning it all up. Burning it all up. Commandant is saying, quick. Tear it down. Make the pile. We are not wanting to leave any nice place for Government to be using if they are coming this side. Soldier is getting kerosene ready from one jerry can and pouring it all over all the palm that is just lying there like dead thing, and then Commandant is coming to me with match and saying to me, you should be lighting the fire. Commandant is making it big honor to be lighting the fire and I am knowing that he is giving it to me only because I am saluting his soldier for him. I am liking very much to be setting fire, but it is still not making me like what he is doing to me last night. Nothing he is giving me is ever making me to like that, but I am not saying it or he will be beating me.

I am taking the match from Commandant and striking them well well until I am hearing SHHKA and seeing the fire on the end of the matchstick. The smell is coming into my nose and making me to want to sneeze. I am holding the match, holding the match until the fire is just eating up the stick and then I am throwing it like that into the pile. The whole place is bursting into big flame but not GBWEM! like if they are bombing or shelling. It is still very hot and still rising up quick quick until everything is burning burning. The flame is having the color of sunset, just orange everywhere, but everything it is touching it is only making them black so quick that there is nothing nice to be looking at. I am not liking the way this orange is just making black smoke to be flying everywhere and if you are looking through it, it is making everything to move back and forward even if it is standing still.

We are all watching for some while and drinking in the smell of the smoke rising up up to the sky. I am watching all the other soldier around us and how everyone is staring at the fire growing bigger and bigger until it is becoming to be very hot and we were also not wanting to be waiting around because the smoke is now beginning to get into our chest and making us to cough and getting into our eye and making us to cry.

Then we are lining up and I am next to Strika waiting to take my place in the truck and watching all the other soldier load up quick quick until the weight is making all the truck to groaning like wounded beast. We are waiting, but before we are getting in, Commandant is coming over and we are saluting him. He is saying to us, no. No. You two are bodyguarding me today. You will be riding in my own car with me.

There are so many of us to be sitting on one seat of Commandant's truck, but we are all squeezing in. Driver is sitting behind the wheel. I am sitting next to driver, Strika is sitting next to me, and Commandant is sitting next to the other door. Inside of Commandant's truck is so nice past anything that all the other soldier are even having. His seat is not made of wood but cushion so it is feeling very nice on your buttom when you are sitting on it. He is having button to be bringing down the window and you can even be turning on the radio when you are driving so we can be listening to music. Driver is turning it on and we are all moving our head up and down like lizard and tapping our finger to the song.

But I am looking out the window too and seeing how thing is just flashing by so fast, WHOOSH there is tree, WHOOSH there is house, WHOOSH there is person, and I am thinking that everything is moving so fast, I will be old man before the war is over. I am knowing I am no more child so if this war is ending I cannot be going back to doing child thing. No. I will be going back to be teachering or farming, or Doctor or Engineer, and I will be finding my mother and my sister, but not my father because he is dying in this war.

My thinking is like the road, going on and on, and on and on, until it is taking me so far far away from this place. Sometimes I am thinking of my life far far ahead and sometimes I am thinking of all the life I am leaving behind. And then I am looking at Commandant and Strika and I am also thinking to myself that both of them are looking so peaceful and beautiful like how we are looking before the war, like how we are being after the war, but not like now. Now we just be looking like animal.

Driving driving and walking walking and driving driving and walking walking and fighting and soldiering and running from road into bush and bush onto road. That is all we are doing. That is the only thing we can be doing until one day we are coming to one town. Commandant is calling it his town because he is living here as soldier sometimes before this war is starting. I am seeing sign that is saying, Welcome to the Town of Abundant Resources. I can read so I am knowing what welcome is meaning. I am knowing what town is meaning. And I am knowing what is abundant resources. But still I am wanting to know what this sign is meaning for us. I am wanting to ask somebody but I am not saying anything. No word is coming out of my mouth.

As we are standing on this road, I am seeing the breezes and feeling the grasses. I am mixing up but I am knowing always to be keeping my mouth closed. I am not saying anything but I am thinking nothing is easy. I am not happying anymore. I am not happying ever again.

Before we are coming here, Commandant is telling me how his town is fine past any other town, that his place is like paradise they are always talking about in Bible. In this place, he is saying, in this place enh. Everything is so fine. If you are looking from the top of hill, you are seeing how all the house is having different color roof, red, green, blue, yellow, orange so the whole place is just looking like field of flower stretching all the way up to the river which is shining shining. Ah, this river is shining so bright at the end of the town like one big piece of tin lying on the ground. We are always saying, he is saying, that in this place, maybe one day, big bird will just be coming down and carrying it off because he is thinking it is tin and not water. And ah ah! Agu, we are always having light all the time, and water and so many foods to be eating like chicken, and cow, and goat, and vegetable, and fruit, any kind fruit you are wanting because trader is always bringing everything he is having to this place to be selling. There is nothing they are not selling in this place. If you are wanting beautiful clothe, you can have clothe. If you are wanting beautiful wood, you can have wood, and jewelry—gold and silver. It is all here. We are having it all. But that is not even what I am really liking.

He is saying, the best thing this town is having is all the womens. Ah, woman in this place is just too beautiful. If you just see woman here, before you are even knowing it, your soldier is standing at full tenshun. They are having breast big like pillow and so nice and round that their clothe is even rejoicing to be holding them. And they are having buttom that is just rounding so nice that anytime they are sitting down, chair is also rejoicing.

They are knowing well well how to make man feel so good with their kissing and loving. He is saying, kai! the last time I am in this place, enh! I am having four womens in one day until my soldier is hurting too much for me to even be easing myself.

You cannot even be knowing how nice this place is. It is just too nice, he is saying. And I am looking at him with my eye so open. So he is saying to me, why are you looking at me with your eye open like that? Enh? You think it is lie? Agu, enh, you think it is lie?

Let me be telling you how town is coming to this place, he is saying. Long long ago, he is saying, but not so long ago that there is no human but before human is really traveling from one village to the next village, there was trader who was just trading small small clothe in his own village. He is greedy man just trying to make his money from anything he is having, so all of the people in his village are living very poor and he is the only one living rich with the biggest compound, the most yam, and the most wife and child than anybody in his village—even the chief.

So one day there was small famine in the whole of the village, not too big but big enough that people are beginning to hungry too much and since it is famine, the land is not even giving anything for them to be eating because the land is hungry itself. So they are coming to the richest Cloth Seller, all of them the whole village in their brown rag and their dry skin. And they are asking him in one big voice that is just weak even though there are so many of them, Please Papa. Please give us food you are storing because we are so hungry and you are so rich. And the Cloth Seller was sweating and looking to his storage and then looking to everybody in the village and saying, why are you asking me for my yam? Are any of you helping my family and me when I am harvesting them? And then all of the village people were hmmming and ahahing between themself because it is all of their monies that is making this man to be so rich that he can be planting so many yam. So everybody in the village was just angrying at this Cloth Seller and shouting that he is not having any heart, and attacking him and his family until the man—who was also coward—is just running running, leaving his family to all the angry people agitating for food.

He was traveling, traveling, traveling through the bush looking left and right, walking for many many day, too many day. No food. No water. All his clothe tearing by the bush and his feets cutting with root and rock in the road until one day he is finding one old woman lying on the road. The woman was having only one eye and no teeths so that you are not even hearing what she is saying too much of the time. Cloth Seller was seeing that she is smelling of food so he was going to her and saying, Mma. Please Mma. Help me. I am just small trader leaving his village for trading, but robber on the road is attacking me and now I am having nothing, not even one drop of water to drink. The old woman he is talking to is witch and she is saying to him, don't worry. If you are helping me to do something, then I will be giving you anything you are wanting. Normal, this man is not really helping to anybody and just trying to help himself, but this time he is hungrying so much that he is listening well well.

Witch is saying, I am old woman just too weak to be moving from my place under this nice tree, but my house is not too too far. Go into my house and be bringing yam pottage I am making, but do not be eating any of it until you are here. So Cloth Seller was following what Witch is saying and finding her hut in the middle of bush. It was smelling so bad like refuses all around and the whole mud of the hut is melting back into the ground because she is only having one leg and not able to be fixing it all the time like you are always having to fix mud hut. He was also smelling yam pottage so he was going into the hut and finding in the middle, on the fire, big bowl of it. At this time, he was hungrying so much that he is sitting down and eating some food for himself. When he was finishing, he was fulling so much that he is lying down his head on the ground and sleeping.

When he is waking up, he was seeing that there was not even very much yam pottage left, so he is very shameful and picking up the pot from the fire and rushing back to Witch thinking, oh my God! What can I be doing? What can I be doing? When he is getting to the place he is leaving Witch, he is saying to her before she is even having chance to speak, Mma please. I am so sorry I am just spilling yam pottage onto the ground that is why there is only small small food left. Please be forgiving me because I am not meaning to do you any harm. Witch is looking at him and saying to him, are you eating well? And he is answering, yes well well. The food is very good, before he is even knowing what he is saying. Then she is looking up at him and saying, ah ah liar. You know that I am Witch and watching you with my one eye I am leaving in my house. And she was shouting on the man. But Cloth Seller was saying to Witch, I am traveling for too many day and I am so hungry and tired. Please.

Please. Please. Witch was saying, that is fine since you are helping me at least have some food. I am sorrying for you and will be giving you one wish before you are moving on. What is it that you are wanting most in this world?

Cloth Seller was just thinking, even having his mouth to watering more when he is hearing this woman saying this thing. How can she, he was asking himself, how can she be asking me this? Then he is saying to her, I can be having anything that I am wanting in this whole world? Anything? And she is saying, yes. Anything. So the man is remembering all of the nice thing he is leaving in his village. All of the nice clothe and food, the nice bed and other thing and then he was saying to her, Mma. Please. If you are giving me anything in the world, then I am wanting all the richness that you can be having in this world. Witch was angrying. She is saying, foolish somebody. Stupid man. All you are thinking about is what you are wanting. She was angrying so much that she is getting up and hopping on her one foot. She is shouting, go on your way. In small small while you will be finding river. Lie down by this river and make your bed and when you are waking up, you will be having everything you are ever wanting.

He is not even saying one more word to Witch. Cloth Seller was rushing off into the bush and after some little time was coming to the bank of great river that was just shining silver with all the sun. He was kneeling down and laughing to himself because he was almost having all of the rich in the world. Then he is finding one rock for his pillow and even though he was too too happy to be sleeping, he was putting his head down and finally, after some time, falling asleep.

This Cloth Seller is never waking up. Instead, he is becoming the market and having everything that anybody can ever be wanting. That is why you can be standing above this town and seeing how it is looking like man lying near the river. And that is why they are saying, you can never be trusting anybody or anything in this town. It is the market. It is having everything, but nothing is ever really how it is looking.

Commandant is telling this to me and I am stopping to open my eye wide wide. I am looking this way and that, just seeing how all of the soldier is agitating and agitating. They are talking about all food and drink and womens they will be finding for this place. As we are moving down the hill into the town, I am seeing market stretching forever and ever swallowing up all of the house and building in this town. Everywhere, the street is full of refuses which are lining the road up and down and smelling like dead body rotting. I am seeing animal leg and head and it is making me to want to vomit even if I am seeing not just dead animal body but dead human body before. This one on the road is making my belly to be turning over. Everywhere we are going, we are seeing refuses, dead animal, and people everywhere. All of the house, if they are looking fine from far away, they are not looking fine anymore close up. They are all looking like old man and woman who is wanting to fall down. Bullet hole is everywhere like bullet is locust and just making their nest in anything around, even concrete. And now, I am seeing how there is small small crater here and there. Sometimes you will just be looking as you are driving—house, house, house, no house, and where there is no more house, the ground is looking like somebody is pressing thumb into it, only the thumb is like giant's thumb. In these place, everything is sometimes shining with broken glass and sometimes you are still smelling the smokes from the rubbles. I am looking to see if anybody but me is looking at this kind thing, but I am the only one looking and thinking, KAI! this is just too very bad. They are all just thinking about all of the drink and woman that we can be getting in this place. I am too young to be knowing about these thing even if I am knowing from how the men are talking about woman that I am really wanting one to be making my soldier feel good. I am wanting one, but not like how we are getting them in battle.

If this town was big place for all of the trader to be buying and selling this and that, I am not seeing it. The market is empty. The whole place is just empty. Too many of the roofs is just falling and showing bullet hole inside of them making me to thinking, how much person are dying here every day? So so much because they are not enough people to be burying all of the dying people. They are just throwing them into the street like refuses.

We are getting out of all the truck and walking, looking for some good thing. I am not knowing if Commandant is telling everybody about all the thing we should be finding in this place. I am thinking he is not because they should be madding since we are not finding any good thing. We are walking through the market and finding nothing. And when we are walking out of the market, we are still finding nothing.

I am looking left to right and left to right at the compound on each side. There is nothing like what Commandant is saying here even if I am beginning to see that there is more life here than I am first thinking. First, I am seeing bony cat licking dusty old chicken bone on the ground. The bone is so dry that it is even looking like rock, like it should be breaking the cat's teeths, but the cat is not minding so much because it is at least feeding small small on the thing it is finding. All of us is then going around one corner and I am finally seeing few person walking around. These people are acting like soldier is nothing new or real to them in this place where in other place everybody is fearing us. I am thinking, what if they are not seeing me? What if they are not seeing us? What if we are dying and becoming spirit? What if they are spirit because they are all looking the same? The people are all looking the same, and I am not knowing who is old and who is young or who is man and who is woman. I am thinking to myself, this place is making me to confuse too much with its kind of people.

I am following behind Commandant and Luftenant and Rambo and Strika. All the other soldier is following behind me. We are turning onto one road that is only just wide enough for us to be moving one man behind the next man, one truck behind the next truck. On each side of us there is building with two or three floor and as we are walking, woman is just looking down at us and I am seeing how they are just holding cloth around their breast like that. Commandant and Luftenant and Rambo and everybody is looking round and round and licking their lip like this is the best thing we are ever seeing. All of the building is behind wall that is crumbling, but they are each having gateman or woman just sitting with stick and looking at us, not smiling. I am hearing one man shouting loud, enhen now! Don't worry. Don't worry baby! We are coming back for you!

It is some time that we are walking and driving like this until Commandant is saying, enhen, and we are stopping in one place. The place we are coming to is just one house that is having no guard or anybody at the gate. We are opening the rusty gate and they is screaming so loud. Behind the gate is one compound where person is not coming for long long time. I am knowing because the grasses are growing very high. I am wondering why Commandant is bringing us here when suddenly I am seeing gun, big gun, the biggest gun I am ever seeing, so big that they are coming with seat so you can be sitting down when you are shooting them. Next to them is big triangle of bullet, bullet even bigger than my arm. These gun are standing on wheel even bigger than my whole body and it is making me to want to go and touch them. All of these bullet and gun is rusting like nobody is even using them for too long. None of us is seeing such thing before.

Commandant is yelling, TENSHUN and I am seeing that now all of us is standing here and all of us is forming tenshun very quickly. Then, Commandant is saying to us that we should be behaving ourself and looking sharp and resting well well that we will be knowing what is happening in some time. Everybody is listening but nobody is really understanding what he is saying about moving to the front and fighting the enemy in this place or that place because I am never seeing this place or that place for my whole life. Anyway, it is not mattering too much because I am just following order and not having to do anything else.

After he is shouting on us like this, he is telling us to dismiss and make our camp.

The rest of the soldier are now going every this way and that way to be seeing what is in this kind of place that we are never seeing before. I am wanting to go especially to all the big gun so I can be seeing if I can sit in them and look at the sky to be shooting, but Commandant is telling me and Strika, follow me. We are going, and he is walking to one house, the only house remaining in this compound.

We are opening the door of this house into room with sunlight that is having many window with all of the glass gone. I am knowing immediately that this place is school because I am seeing bench, and table, and blackboard, only every place is having so many many map with green pin, and yellow pin, and blue pin, and white pin, everywhere. These map is covering every place on the wall and table and also sometimes the floor. My head is spinning this way and that way because I am feeling like I am inside the world and I am looking at how everything must look from the inside instead of outside. It is not map of the world, but map of my country so everywhere is name of place I am hearing sometimes there is fighting or place where I am hearing there is the enemy one day and no enemy the next day, but I am not knowing that everywhere there is war. I am looking at this pin and that pin and thinking, if I am to run away where can I be running to? Where can I be running to? War is everywhere. My heart is beating so fast and I am sweating so much. I am wanting to sit down.

Suddenly, I am standing here in this room, but I am also

standing in my classroom in the shadow, in the corner like what is happening when you are talking too much or if you are not doing your lesson proper. I am seeing all of the face I am knowing from home all sitting there and doing work and then I am looking at the woman who is writing lesson on the board. She is stepping like she is having limp, but her body is looking like Mistress Gloria. She is writing, I will not kill, I will not kill. I will not kill, and everybody is writing in their book, I will not kill, I will not kill excepting me because I am not having book. Then the teacher is turning around and looking at me and I am fearing because she is having the face of that woman I am killing with blood everywhere on her face and in her eye. She is saying to me, are you not understanding our lesson, even while she is walking to me with one sharp machete that is shining like the river is shining. When she is coming near to me, all of the face of the child are only the girl that they are using anyhow, that Strika is killing. I am starting to want to scream.

AGU!

I am hearing my name and then everything is map and I am standing inside the world looking at Commandant just looking at me. I am saying, yes Sah! Yes Sah! I am shouting and standing tenshun and trying to look like I am prouding and strong.

He is saying to me, what is wrong? What is wrong? But I am not answering. My mouth is shut. Then he is saying, come on. Let us leave this place.

Outside it is getting dark, but the whole compound is starting to grow with noise because they are preparing meal. Each one soldier is talking to the next, talking talking. I am listening to them, but I am also thinking of all of the map and all of the fighting that is going on in this whole world and I am fearing for my life. I am thinking if there is even any way to be getting out.

When it is dark, we are not even lighting match or the enemy may be finding where we are and sending helicopter and plane to be bombing and shooting us. Everywhere is just black, but you are hearing voice just talking or singing like spirit in the night. Everywhere you are going you are hearing different talking different story, different song. We are not just like army now, we are like school or family is what I am thinking. Each person is finding his own best friend and they are going off to this corner or that corner. I am walking around to be seeing if I can find Strika, but each step I am taking is so slow and each time I am stepping I am having to put my hand in front of me to be finding my way. This darkness is so full like it is my mother's hug. Heya! I am remembering my mother and how she is so good to me that each time she is hugging me that is all I am needing to see the dark skin of her arm holding me close to her and I am knowing that the life I am living is so good. This kind of dark is making me to feel like I am turning inside out, so all of my thought is floating outside of me and all of my clothe is inside of me. I am walking with my hand stretching out in front of me because I am trying to catch all of those thought that is floating around me so I can make sure no part of me is missing.

I am walking in the direction I am remembering where is the building. As I am walking to the building, I am hearing sound from before the war when I am in school, sound of laughter and sound of crying and sound like the game we are playing during school break. I am hearing sound of pencil writing on paper and sound of chalk writing on blackboard and how eraser is sounding when I am beating it on the stone to be removing the dust. I am hearing how all the girl is tearing paper to be passing note back and forward and how all the boy is just whispering this answer and that answer so we can be beating all the girl. I am hearing sound of lizard watching us from the wall and mosquito entering the classroom making it so hard to be hearing what the teacher is saying. I am hearing the sound of Dike chewing gum or licking sweet when we are not supposed to be eating anything. I am hearing sound of my sandal tapping on the ground when I am doing my maths until Mistress Gloria is telling us, lesson is over and now it is time to go home. I am hearing the prayer we are saying each day at the end of all the lesson, please God help me to use what I have learned for the good of all when I go home. I am hearing all of this thing and it is making me to sad.

Commandant is smoking cigarette on the step of the house when I am walking up. He is alone and staring up to the sky. Each time he is smoking, he is holding his cigarette down so that nobody can be seeing the light. I am hoping he is not seeing me or saying anything to me even though I am coming right close to him, but then it is like he is animal knowing something is there even if he is not seeing it and he is shouting, AGU! AH AGU! WHAT ARE YOU DOING? JUST COME HERE RIGHT NOW. And when I am coming he is saying softly softly, sit down sit down. So I am sitting down, but is like he cannot even be seeing that I am sitting there next to him, like the darkness between us is too much. I am just drinking the smoke from his own cigarette and wishing that I had not been giving my own away for small small biscuit because I am still so hungry. After he is finishing smoking his cigarette to the end, until the spot of fire is just disappearing and his face is not shining orange anymore, he is putting his hand on my head and rubbing his rough hand on the back of my neck. Sometimes Agu, I am thinking he is saying to me, sometimes I am feeling sorry for you. I am looking at him, but I cannot be seeing anything on his face because it is too dark. But he is not saying, sometimes Agu, I am feeling sorry for you. I am wishing he is saying something like that, but he is never saying anything like that to me. He is moving closer to me and I am slowly moving away from him and we are doing this on the verandah of the school building until Luftenant is calling out to us, Commandant Sah. Is that you? And is that Agu? Commandant is saying, let us go. Hmm. If you are my bodyguard, then if I am going, you are also going. Is it not so?

Commandant is saying we are going out this night. He is saying to all the soldier, half of you come on, let us go, and then dividing us into half. To the other half, he is saying, you should be staying here. When they are grumbling, he is saying, don't worry. There is enough woman so that they will still be here tomorrow. Relax yourself enh. I am walking with Commandant and Luftenant as they are talking about drink and money and womens and talking talking about how nice it is. We are moving very slowly in the road because we cannot be using any light. Around me, all the men are smelling hungry, like they will be chopping something sweet very soon. Even if I have been eating too much food this night, my stomach is feeling hungry and more hungry each time we are turning one corner on the road. There is no way to be seeing where we are going at all at all. No house is having light. No house is even having lamp or candle, and the whole place is like death's hometown.

We are stopping beside wall of concrete, the wall of one compound. Commandant is stamping his feets on the ground and spitting between his boot and cursing. There is woman at the gate just sitting on stool with her head in her hand and dog that is grumbling at her feets when we are coming close. She is shining torchlight very quickly in our eye and saying, so you have come enh? One other man is saying, why are you so angry Sista? And then she is looking at me and saying, child is not coming for this place. Stupid woman, I am starting to abuse her, but Commandant is hitting my head and saying, he is my own bodyguard. She is nodding and spitting at me and it is landing just next to my feets, but it is not touching me. Devil bless you, she is saying, but I am just walking by.

Inside of the compound is smaller than where we are camping, but there is large house inside. I am hearing the sound of generator in this compound, but I am not seeing any light anywhere. We are entering into the house, into room that is just having blue light everywhere. All of the table and chair and everything is just looking blue, and even my skin and Commandant's skin is looking blue and black like we are already dead. Woman is coming up to us and her eye is shining like blue diamond. She is limping so when she is stepping this way and that way her slipper is just making step slap like she is beating the floor because she is angry with it. Every time she is stepping, all the fly is jumping from the table and drink and cup that are just everywhere making whole place to be smelling of beer and alcohol. Also, from the corner of the room behind big tower of bread loaf piled high on each other to the roof like cement block is coming the smell of burning meat and nice-tasting stew. From the roof is hanging flag of different beer and mineral like they are country that everybody should be visiting. They are not flying back and forward like normal flag and instead are just hanging down like they are not even wanting to be on the wall. On all of the window there is heavy board and heavy black cloth making sure that there is no light even allowed to come out, but because there is no open window, the whole place is just heating too much. We are all filling up the room and just looking. I am hearing this sound like mosquito that is when I am looking up and seeing television. TELEVISION! In this war! Can you imagine? There is no sound coming from it, but one movie is playing. I am having to try and hear what they are saying, but I am seeing police officer and woman who is looking like prostitute shouting at each other on the screen. A whole television! I am never even seeing anything like this since war is starting.

Mma. Bring something that will satisfy soldier, Commandant is shouting at the woman and the other men are just laughing. Bring beer! Bring mineral! Bring it all! Commandant is shouting.

It is only now that I am seeing woman who is looking very young and very nice just sitting on one stool in the back of the room. The Madam is shouting at her, get up you lazy idiot can't you see we are having guest and this young woman is getting up and going to the cooler. She is bending down so her buttom is just rising high into the air. I am seeing Commandant and the other men now just looking looking and not even moving their eye from this buttom like it is piece of cooked meat. Then they are laughing to each other, heye! Ekaa ekaa ekaa. Heye! Kehi, kehi, kehi. When the girl is turning around I am seeing how sweat is just soaking her white head tie which is really looking blue because of the light. She is breathing out and opening her mouth so that her lip are blowing small bubble of spit into the air. It is all warm, she is saying. No ice to be cooling it, and Commandant is angrying, no ice. How can that be enh? Because of war, the woman is saying. Ah ah! War no stop you from making ice. Bring the drink. We will be drinking it even if it is warm, Commandant is saying. And when the girl is coming over, it is like he is just changing so when she is near he is sticking his hand out to be touching her all over. Baby, he is saying, baby, I love you when he is touching her buttom. She is not liking it. The other men are just laughing laughing and looking at her breast which is even showing because there is so much sweat in her shirt. I am looking at her breast also and my soldier is becoming to stand at tenshun which is making me to feel good and it is not making me to feel good. Madam, I am saying to this young woman while they are laughing and now drinking their warm drink, Madam be bringing us some breads. The woman is sucking in her teeths at me. Is this war just making you to have no respect for your elder? This small thing borned yesterday trying to order me around. Enh! You this small thing. I can be your mother! The men are laughing so loud that the fly is jumping in the blue light, but she is still getting breads and bringing it back. When she is coming back, Commandant is even grabbing her breast and she is slapping him on the hand, but he and the men are still smiling.

The big Madam is just watching from one corner until she is growing angry and saying if it is woman you are wanting, leave this one. I am having plenty plenty womens in the back if you are having plenty plenty money to be giving me. And just like that they are all getting up and following the big Madam through door in the back of the room just leaving me to be sitting here with the warm drink and this breads that the young woman is throwing at me. I am waiting. Ten minute. Twenty minute just staring at the television and the movie with policeman and prostitute. I am chewing my breads and also watching the young woman who is coming over to collect the bottle on the table. I am looking at her breast and wanting to touch her buttom like Commandant is doing, but as soon as I am even bringing up my hand to be touching her, she is looking at me like she will be beating me to death and sucking in her teeths so I am putting my hand down. Then I am getting so hot because there is not even one bit of air in this room and I am going outside to be catching some breath.

When I am sitting outside in the dark, under the window, I am hearing all of these noise coming from inside sounding just like Commandant when he is entering me. I am hearing these thing and it is making my soldier to become very hard and I am not knowing what to be doing. I am touching it very softly through my short and it is feeling very good, so I am touching it some more whenever I am hearing the man and woman making more sound from the room. My hand is just moving up and down and up and down like it is not even part of my body anymore and I am thinking to myself of how I will be touching breast and leg. All of this thing is making my eye to close and my heart to beat fastly and I am liking it and doing it so much until I am just hearing one scream, AYIIIEEE!!!! SHE HAS KILLED ME OH!

And then I am hearing all of this footstep running this way and that in house, so I am stopping to touch myself and I am running inside to the room with the blue light where I am finding that all of the soldier are coming out of their room just looking like something is confusing them. Then I am seeing how Luftenant is just holding the wall and having blood to be coming from his mouth shining black in the blue light. I am looking at him and thinking whatever it is that is happening is good for him, but then I am seeing how his face is looking like all the bad thing in the world is paining him and I am sorrying small small. All of the other soldier is coming up to him and they are holding him by one arm or the other arm and helping him to sit down in chair. Commandant is coming out of the back door only wearing his short and his soldier is still at full tenshun when he is yelling, WHAT IS IT THAT IS HAPPENING! Everybody is looking at Luftenant and then looking at woman who is also coming out of the room after Luftenant. She is bleeding from her body where it is looking like somebody is beating her in the head and beating her in the mouth. She cannot even be walking at all so she is holding the wall when she is trying to move and also holding one hand to her neck. Nobody is knowing what to do until the Madam is coming out and asking what is happening. And then the other woman are coming out from their room, some of them wearing one cloth and trying to cover their body while other is just walking out like that, naked, like it is no problem to be walking around with no clothe.

All of the soldier are looking at Luftenant who is pointing to his stomach. What is happening, one man is asking. And then they are lying Luftenant on the table under the television and making him to stretch out. KAI! someone is shouting. Enh? another is saying and they are all looking down at Luftenant's body. I am going over to see what I can be seeing, and then I am seeing how he is just having one knife sticking out from his belly just like that. It is making me to grab my own belly just to be making sure that everything is still there. Luftenant is not even screaming anymore. He is just shaking shaking on the table and mumbling to himself like he is madman.

Commandant is shouting, WHO IS DOING THIS? And then the Madam is coming and saying, heyeye now! What is happening here oh? She is looking at her girl who is just bleeding and crying, and holding her throat, and coughing, he is just grabbing my neck and beating me, so what am I supposed to be doing? I am only small girl. How can I be stopping him from doing anything? So I am just seeing this knife that he is having in his trouser and I am using it and just chooking him to get him off of me. I am not knowing it is going to be like this. I am watching how Commandant's face is darking and how the whole room is smelling of fear and sweat. I am thinking that he will be telling us to be grabbing this woman and shooting her, but he is not even opening his mouth. He is just standing there and looking around us and then at Luftenant who is lying shaking shaking on the table. COME ON! Everybody just get up! Get him up! Let us be getting out of here, he is saying and looking at the big Madam who is just holding her girl and using cloth to be wiping the blood from her face. No woman is even saying anything because they are fearing too much. COME ON! MOVE QUICK! Commandant is shouting and then he is going into the back room to be getting his clothe on and all of the other soldier are taking turn to be doing the same. Then we are picking up Luftenant and carrying him out of this building and into the night. The woman at the gate is sleeping like she is not even knowing anything is happening at all inside and nobody is telling her anything because the men are just trying to be keeping their soldier between their leg and their trouser from falling down.

A whole three day we are staying here and Luftenant is not getting better. Every day somebody is washing his stomach with cloth and water and soap, but it is not doing anything and he is just shivering in the night. We are keeping him in the building in our camp because that way the mosquito is not getting to him as easily, and since it is not too many people walking this way and that we are not having to worry that the building will be falling down. Three whole day somebody is watching him on and off and on and off, but he is never speaking anymore and his face is just growing too white.

We are kneeling around his bed, squeezing brown water

onto his face and shining kerosene lamp into his eye. And his eye is so wide we are seeing through to the back of his head. All the morning, he is just groaning and moaning like his spirit is fighting to be let free from his body and all the evening, he is shaking and shivering like it is so cold even though the night is so hot that we are all sweating. We are just watching him like this for all this time and everybody is not saying anything.

It is taking Luftenant three whole day to be dying, and then he is dying when the moon is full and the night is shining like silver. We are dumping his body in the gutter—me, Strika, Commandant, and Rambo—but before that, Rambo is just taking his clothe because Commandant is saying that Rambo is new Luftenant. Then we are leaving his body for the cat and dog and maggot and worm to eat. We are leaving him and I am thinking that he is getting his wish not to be fighting anymore, and I am fearing because I am seeing that the only way not to be fighting is to die. I am not wanting to die.

It is night. It is day. It is light. It is dark. It is too hot. It is too cold. It is raining. It is too much sunshine. It is too dry. It is too wet. But all the time we are fighting. No matter what, we are always fighting. All the time bullet is just eating everything, leaf, tree, ground, person—eating them—just making person to bleed everywhere and there is so much blood flooding all over the bush. The bleeding is making people to be screaming and shouting all the time, shouting to father and to mother, shouting to God or to Devil, shouting one language that nobody is really knowing at all. Sometimes I am covering my ear so I am not hearing bullet and shouting, and sometimes I am shouting and screaming also so I am not hearing anything but my own voice. Sometimes I am wanting to cry very loud, but nobody is crying in this place. If I am crying, they will be looking at me because soldier is not supposed to be crying.

All the time, we are sick and going to toilet, shitting water. We are hungry too and living off anything we can find. Lizard, we are eating them. Insect, we are eating them or even better, if we are finding them, we are eating rat and every other kind of bush animal. Sometimes we are eating this leaf or that leaf, but leaf is what is always making my belly to turn so I am not eating it so much. Meat is also making my stomach to turn because we are not able to use too much fire to cook it because if we are using too much fire, then the enemy will be seeing us and shooting us dead from where they are hiding. I am always hungry, so hungry that I am always dreaming of chicken and how I will be eating it, how I will be crunching its beak and eating even the feather. I am so hungry I can be eating wood if it is making me to hungry less, but it is only hurting my belly and making me to vomit and shit. I am so hungry I can even be eating my skin small by small if it is not making me to bleed to death. I am so hungry that I am wanting to die, but if I am dying, then I will be dead.

But there is so much bombing and bombing and shelling and shelling and sending helicopter to come and shine light on us and kill us. All the time, the ground is shaking and the tree is shaking and the air is smelling of smoke or the air is beating in your ear BOTU BOTU BOTU and you are not even having one second to be thinking anything. So much time pass us now. I am not seeing road or village or woman or children for too long. I am only seeing war, one evil spirit sitting in the bush just having too much happiness because all the time he is eating what he wants to eat—us—and seeing what he is wanting to see— killing—so he is just laughing GBWEM! GBWEM! GBWEM!

All of our truck is gone, just bombed away, so we are having to walk everywhere now, and there is not so many of us any- more. People are just dying like this every day. One boy named

Hope is dying, just burning up in the fire of bomb that is hitting truck. One man we are calling Dagger is dying because he is stepping on mine and it is just chewing his whole body to many piece like termite is chewing wood. And Griot is dying from malaria making him to shaking shaking, and Preacher is dying holding his Bible in one hand and his leg in the other screaming to God, come take me come take me. People are dying just like that every day. Everyone I am knowing is dying. And even all the soldier whose name I am not knowing is dying. In the middle of this war, I am even missing some of them. I am even missing some of them.

Commandant is helping some people to be dying. Already he is shooting three people he is calling traitor, including Driver who is trying to run away because he is having no more truck to be driving. After Commandant is shooting Driver, he is laughing laughing and talking to himself and not even listening to anyone. Not even Rambo who is new Luftenant. When I am seeing all of this, all of this bombing bombing, killing killing, and dying dying, I am thinking to myself that now, as we are in this bush, only ant is still making and living. I am wishing I am ant.

Now we are just living underground in trench that we are digging in the red mud and just living inside it like one kind of snake or rat. When it is dry, we are happying because there is no water anywhere and we can just be fighting war. When it is raining, ah! It is so terrible. So terrible. It is like living in gutter. Sometimes water is coming up to my belly and I am just looking at my reflection staring at me everywhere I am going. We are staying in this place for too long. I am tired and hungry and I am wanting to leave.

There is so much mist that is wrapping around people like extra shirt. No shooting still for today and I am wanting to think, HEYA! WAR IS OVER! WAR IS OVER! but then I am thinking, is it really over? This whiteness that is hanging around all of us and making it hard to breathing is making me to feel like somebody is wanting to fly into my chest and close my nose with cotton. My feets are staying in the water all night so I am feeling they are curling at the end like the feets of rat. Some of the men are sleeping and hugging themself against the wall of the trench with their shirt on their head to be protecting them from the rain. They are shivering because there is cool wind that is coming through the whole place. It is hard not to be stepping on them because they are just appearing quickly quickly from the mist. One second everything is all white around me and then I am kicking foot that is just appearing and the man is screaming in his sleep but not waking up. I am learning to see where the heat from body is making it less thick so I am walking carefully when I am seeing this. Some of the men are awake because they are on guard all night and I am moving gegerly gegerly to not be disturbing them.

Strika is standing outside Commandant's HQ which is only just the trench, but with one blue cloth covering with leaf so he is not getting as wet as the rest of us. Strika is holding gun that is so heavy in his hand it is pulling the right side of his body to the ground. We are looking at each other for long time and then I am bringing my hand to be beating away the mist. I am not liking

Strika's eye because they are too red and his teeths because th
are too brown and his head because it is big, but he is my fri
even if he is looking ugly. He is giving me the gun and
walking past me.

I am stepping inside HQ to see Commandant sleeping on his
crate with his back against the mud wall and his boot stretching
into the muddy water. Cigarette and ash is floating in the water
around him and the whole room is smelling of smoke. I am taking deep breath to be drinking it all in because it is somehow
making my body to full so I am not feeling as hungry.

His beard is growing so thick now that it is almost covering
his whole chin and cheek. When he is breathing out, the hairs is
shaking with his breath. Commandant is looking like wild man
and behaving like madman. I am thinking of him running naked
through the bush with only his big beard reaching down to his
feets and it is making me want to laugh, but I am too hungry.
Laughing is making my belly to hurt too much. Commandant is
fearing the other soldier so much now that he is saying it is
always good to be sleeping with one eye open. That is why
either Strika or myself is always standing outside when he is
sleeping. I am his one eye. Strika is his other.

Come on. Out of my way, Rambo's head is following his
voice out of the mist while his spit is spraying onto my face. He
is stepping from the whiteness to stand right in front of me. I am
seeing him with his gun hanging on his shoulder. My belly is
tighting and my neck is becoming stiff. I am holding the gun
Strika is giving to me.

Commandant is sleeping, I am saying to Rambo. Well wake

him up, he is saying back. I am stepping in front of him and kicking water in his boot. He is tiring so don't be bothering him, I am saying. My leg is shaking shaking and my feets are too too cold. Out of my way, Rambo is saying again and stepping right so I am holding my gun tighter and stepping in front of him. His boot is squishing the mud. No he is resting, I am saying.

Rambo is bending down so I am seeing his face and his beard that is growing thick and black. Listen you small boy. Get out of the way. We are not playing game. I am not remembering the last time I am playing game.

What is all of this noise, Commandant is saying. Sah it is me, Rambo is answering. Idiot can't you see I am sleeping. Enhen now Sah I can see. Then shutup and go back to your post. No Sah I am not doing that anymore Sah. And why not? Because we are leaving Sah. WHO AND WHO IS LEAVING? Commandant is shouting and then I am hearing him laughing quietly to himself from the shadow of his HQ.

In front of me, Rambo is swallowing so hard that I am feeling it in my own throat. And from the back of the HQ, Commandant's laughing is growing louder and louder until I am feeling him standing right behind me. He is pushing me aside with his arm and I am hitting rock in the wall. My shoulder is beginning to hurt. Who is leaving. Idiot. Go back to your post. You are leaving when I say leave. Understood? No Sah, never, Rambo is saying. We are going, Rambo is saying. I no want trouble oh, he is saying. Who is this we enh, Commandant is saying and laughing. You are the only one stupid enough—I AM GOING, one voice is shouting. I AM GOING TOO. AND

ME, AND ME, AND ME, the voice keep yelling from the mist softer and softer until the farthest person is shouting small small, saying and me. Rambo is sliding his finger to the trigger of his gun and I am sliding my finger to my own trigger because I am fearing what Commandant will be doing to me if I am not protecting him, but then I am remembering how much he is hurting me when he is chooking me and I am saying never. Never will I be feeling sorry for him. Never will I be helping him. I am lowering my gun.

See! We are going, Rambo is shouting to Commandant. Then he is just taking his gun and shooting him. Only one shot just right in the chest and I am seeing Commandant looking down to his chest with his whole mouth open like he is screaming. But no sound is coming out. He is not saying anything. And then his body is just falling and making the water that is running down the trench red like that.

Rambo is stopping his shaking and is puffing out his chest. Rambo is looking at me and I am looking at him. He is looking at me for long time and then he is just turning and climbing up wall and I am hearing his boot crunching the leaf near my head. Then I am looking up and hearing how all of the soldier is climbing up out of the trench and I am hearing Rambo shouting, COME ON! COME ON QUICK QUICK QUICK! MOVE FAST OH! MOVE WITH SPEED! HOME HOME! WE ARE GOING HOME! I am looking at Commandant and then I am climbing out of the trench. I am tired and hungry and I am wanting to go home.

Commandant is dead. It was so easy to be killing him. Why we are not doing it before I am not knowing, but I am not wanting to think about that right now. I am tiring too much.

We are walking the whole night on this road, left right, left right, left right, left right, and carrying everything we are having, gun, knife, clothe, but that is it because we are not having anything else. How can we be having anything else if we are staying in the bush for so long? I am so tired that it is hard for me to move my leg, but I am following Rambo. So are all the other, just following following even if Rambo is not having map like Commandant. No one person is even marching, left right, left right, like soldier and instead they are just walking almost right almost left, dragging this foot and that foot on the ground. My slipper is sticking to my feets because they are so worn down and almost spoiling, and my feets are paining me because my skin is just rotting and peeling away from too much time standing in the water in the trench. I am feeling like I am always walking on nail and I am wanting to stop to be resting, but nobody is stopping. Strika is not stopping even if his face is cracking everywhere and all his body is just shaking shaking the whole time so I am just moving on almost left almost right, and saying that if he is doing it, then I am also doing it. Sometimes I am falling to the back and then I am getting to fear very much because the man fronting me is like shadow, not person, so I am running to the front which is making my leg to pain even more. I am wishing that I am having boot or canvas shoe so my feets is not hurting. Or even I am wanting to be having car to be driving away so when we are walking I am always hearing car in my head and it is making me to look from side to side for car that is coming to rescue me and take me home. No car. I am thinking I am car and trying to make my feets to move like wheel that is never stopping, but I cannot. I am hungry and I want to stop and rest and eat.

Wherever we are going the moon is following us. It is so big and so bright that we are not using any torch to be seeing, so nobody is fearing that the enemy can be seeing us from wherever they may be hiding in this bush. They cannot see us if we are not having torch because we are invisible unless they are bringing helicopter to be beating the air BOTU BOTU and to be shining their bright light on the road. I see tree and its shadow. I see rock and its shadow and then I am saying let me just make it to that tree or to that rock. My eye is becoming used to the light and I am beginning to see more of everything that is around— each tree, each rock, each piece of rubbish or plant growing alone in the mud of the road. Wherever we are going it is only the moon shining and it is making the whole place to be looking like it is glass and will just break if you are touching it too hard.

I am not liking this at all at all. If something is making of glass, then it is looking nice and beautiful, but it is also looking dead even if it is really having life. Everything here is looking dead when it is really alive. The grass on the side of the road, the tree behind the grasses, my arm or leg, Strika's face, Rambo's neck— they are all looking dead and making me to wonder how all of these dead thing can even be living. I am seeing each thing on the road—I am seeing them all stiff like glass, but I am not able to be seeing through them and I am knowing that the world is full of people and thing even if we are trying to look like they are not there.

I am hearing song. Someone is singing it. It is old song that my mother was singing all the time she is cooking or washing. A song! A song! I am not even hearing music for so long not even from bird. Hearing this music is making my whole skin to burn and I am wanting to scratch myself, my whole self, all over. I feel like I am wanting to dance, but is my body even remembering how? I don't think so. I am sadding because of this. What is happening to the music and all the song we are having? I don't know. I don't know.

I am walking faster because I am trying to see who it is that is singing the song so I can be standing next to him and feeling this music. I am walking from this person to that person, but I am not seeing any sort of sound coming from their mouth. I am feeling like I should be going to that person who is singing and taking all of the sound so I can be having it for myself to be keeping in my pocket for whenever it is getting to be too too bad, but the sound I am looking for is coming from nowhere. I don't mind at all, because the song is making my body to move and I am not having to think anymore. I am having to think of other thought that are just jumping into my head. I am not even minding the gun that is making my whole back to hurt even though it is very heavy. I am thinking of home. How many time am I thinking of my home when we are in the bush? How many time am I seeing all of the people that I am growing up with running around in my head like child running around after school, running to the house, running to the church, running to the market like there is no war and everything is just fine? In my head, all of the people that I am seeing in my home are too too happy and I am thinking, if this is how they are living, why am I staying here to just be walking to someplace not even knowing if I am to be living or dying? I don't know. I don't know.

We are tiring so so much, but we are trying to reach some place. Where is this place? I am not knowing, but I am knowing that Rambo is saying we should not be stopping. So we are not stopping and we are walking through the whole night into the day. The sun is rising behind us so all our shadow is growing front from our feets and making the road ahead very dark which is making it harder to be taking each next step. On this road, it is so empty and I am thinking where have all the people gone because I am not liking the quiet and I am not liking how the only sound in the daytime is the sound of my slipper hitting my own feets, the sound of my breathing so hard every time this is happening because it is paining too much. I cannot be stopping and so I keep walking. I am picking one noise, even if it is just one person moaning, and I am saying that I should be catching that noise so each time the noise is getting softer, I am walking faster to be catching it wherever it is going. They cannot be leaving me behind because I am not knowing where I would be going to in this bush. Just imagine if they are leaving me for the bush and then I am being eaten by animal or other soldier who is sacrificing me to be winning this war. I am thinking about the kind of animal that will be following me if they are leaving me. It is having the body of lion and the head of soldier with helmet and eye that are looking like bullet and teeths that are looking like knife to be chewing me up. Its tail is like gun and its breath like fire that is cooking me well well before it is sitting down to be eating all of the burning part of my body. When this is coming to my head, I am hurrying up my step so that I am not being the last one in the line.

My sweat is burning my eye away. Now it is so hot because the sun is beating on my back and making my gun to warm so much that it is feeling like hot iron on my back. I know it is making mark and burning my back so I am like cow and belonging to one owner which is gun. I am sadding when I am feeling this gun in my back because I am thinking that first when this war is starting, I am wanting gun because I can be using it to protect myself. At this time, gun is belonging to me and it is going wherever I am carrying it, but now it is just riding on my back like it is king and I am servant to be doing whatever it says. If it is saying go right, then my body is walking to the right even if I am struggling to go left, and if it is saying for me to stop, then I am stopping to catch breath, and if I am going down the hill with the other men, then it is saying go faster and it is pushing me down the hill just like that. I am not liking this at all at all and I am wanting to be throwing gun away into the bush, but if I am throwing gun away, then Rambo will be throwing me away because gun is more important than me. I am always remembering this.

The road is too long, but sometimes it is nice to be looking at. I am liking how it is just rising up and down like one animal, how it is moving with the land that it is sitting on. If you are seeing this road in sunshine, then you will be knowing how great it is and how all of the tree is even respecting it and not trying to grow in it. It is only small small thing on the road that are not respecting it, like small plant and sometimes small animal here and there that is getting run over by car and being left there for long time. I am fearing because there is nothing on road excepting us and these small plant that is not respecting road, and if they are not respecting road and road is killing them, then because we are not respecting road from going to toilet and spitting everywhere on it, I am fearing that it may be killing us soon also.

When we are walking, my mouth is tasting of salt, of so much salt that I am not liking the way that salt is tasting anymore. It is making me to thirsty so much and this is even worse than to be hungrying so much because it is making my head to turn from one place to another and the whole world is just spinning round and round me like I am walking in circle. One time I am seeing Strika in front of me walking slowly slowly then the next time I am seeing him behind me walking fastly fastly. This is making me to think am I mad.

We are moving always moving because that is what we are
doing and watching all the thing on the road passing us by.
House, tree, school, empty car all burned up, refuses, all passing
us, but still we are not seeing person. We are coming into another
village, but it is just small, not even really village. It is only just
house on each side of the road, and it is empty, nothing there
excepting the refuses. Person is running away from us like we
are sickness, like we are the most evil thing to be on this earth. I
am looking at road that is cracking in many place like somebody
is just taking it and stretching it until you are seeing the red mud
bleeding from underneath. And everywhere there is rubbishes
just moving along the road like they are people just moving
moving when they are having nothing to be doing. We are just
moving until Strika is stepping on piece of breaking-up bottle
glass and falling down. He is not saying word, not even crying
or screaming. It is not even like he is feeling any pain, but I am
feeling pain for him and it is making me to want to shout and
yell. The other soldier are just walking by us and not even looking at us. Strika. Strika, I am saying. We are having to go or they
will be leaving us. But he is not listening to me. Instead he is just
taking his foot and picking away all of the skin until the glass is
just coming out from his foot. Then he is just licking his finger
clean of all the blood and the dust but making sure to not be
touching any of the sore that is on his lip. He is stretching his
hand out to me and we are getting up and walking. One step.
Two step. He is falling down. Why is Strika doing like this? We
have to be going now, but he is not getting up. Get up! He is just
looking at me and coughing until he is spitting onto the ground

next to him, blood and spit, so much blood. I am asking Strika to be getting up, but he is not listening and he is not getting up. His lip is moving, but there is no noise coming out. I am looking at him. His face is just shining shining like he is sweating so much, but there is no sweat coming out. I am kneeling down on the road next to him just watching all the other soldier walking away from us. I am feeling his heart that is just beating beating like whole village is stomping on the ground. Ah ah! Strika, I am saying. Ah ah! What is happening? But no word is coming from his mouth. His eye is blinking, my eye is blinking and I am seeing him crumpling up. I am getting up and pretending to be walking away. Don't leave me, he is saying and looking at me. And I am shouting at him, come on! Get up and stop this thing you are doing! I am hearing, don't leave me. Please Agu. Don't just be leaving me. Strika is saying something. Enh! Strika is saying something! I am stopping to move, turning around and looking at him and he is looking at me, but it is like he is not even seeing me.

I am bending down to him and seeing his body which is almost just disappearing beneath his clothe. His face is just looking so terrible because all of his skin is just coming away, and his eye is rolling up into his head and showing yellow and red everywhere like going to toilet and blood. Strika is just looking like one piece of refuses on this road. I am trying to be crying, but no tear is coming out from my eye, and I am trying not to be fearing, but Strika—Strika is my brother and my family and the only person I can be talking to even if he is never talking back until now. I am watching him and then I am looking up because

I am not hearing all the other soldier walking on this road. I am not wanting to be left behind. I am not wanting to leave Strika behind. Strika, I am calling his name. Strika, but he is not answering. He is not saying anything. I am saying, Strika? Strika? Strika?

Nothing is the same anymore. I am not being able to be sleeping at all when it is time to sleep. Each time I am lying down my head, some voice inside of me is shouting and starting to make too much trouble so I cannot even be closing my eye. And all of the time this is happening I am fearing that I am not knowing myself anymore. If it is day, I am sitting and staring at the sun like it is the only thing to look at in this world. I am watching how sometime it is bright and other time it is like it is just struggling too much to be shining and I am wanting to ask it why it is even thinking to shine on this world. If I am sun, I will be finding another place to be shining where people are not using my light to be doing terrible terrible thing. At night I am staring at the moon and looking to see if a man is smiling. They are saying man is living there and smiling, but I am never finding anything at all. Nobody is smiling in this place. If it is night, if it is day, nobody is smiling.

So many time I am saying to myself that I will be running away, far far away to where no one can be finding me or seeing me and I will be staying there to the end of time when God is coming to judge the dead and the living. So many time I am telling this to myself, but when I am getting up to go and run away, I am thinking about all the animal and the spirit in the bush, and I am remembering the map which I am seeing in the town and thinking to myself, how can I be running if I am not knowing the way to be taking me away from the war. All I can be doing is sitting here and dreaming about how my leg will carry me far and fast like I am standing and it is the world that is moving to help me. I am dreaming this so many time, but I am waiting for it to happen.

One day we are on the road and then we are just hearing some noise like truck and then we are scattering into the bush, all of us to one side just moving moving quickly into the shadow of all the tree and leaf, just stepping on this branch and that rock running running so that whoever it is will not be seeing us and maybe killing us. I am running running and not looking at where I am putting my feets until KPWAWA, I am just hitting something and my body is falling down KPWOM just like that on the ground. My knee is paining me because I am falling hard and I am looking down to be seeing what is tripping me too easily. I am seeing one dead body just lying on the ground as if he is sleeping. The man is stiff and his whole belly is big like he is fulling of gas. It is so big that it is pressing on the button of his uniform until it is looking like it is going to pop. I am just looking down at this man because something is telling me in my head that this is meaning that we are getting closer to the war.

One soldier is also seeing this dead body and then he is coming and kneeling down next to him and unbuttoning the shirt. There is insect all over. Shiny beetle with silver on its back and little white maggot is just crawling up and down this dead man's chest. Then the man is turning the body over and taking off the shirt and rolling it up and putting it under his arm. He is going to the leg and removing the boot from it and putting his own slipper on the man's feets. He is looking at me and smiling and showing his brown teeths and then he is quickly running away to be joining the other soldier. I am watching him running away and I am wanting to be getting up and running after him because I do not want to be staying in this place with one dead body. But my leg is not getting up. I am just thinking thinking and I am asking to myself, why, if I am killing man and woman and beating them until their blood is just covering my whole body, if I am seeing my friend just sitting down by the road and shaking like Devil is possessing him, why am I wanting to cry and vomit if I am only seeing dead body?

And then I am thinking of all the thing I am doing. If they are ordering me KILL, I am killing, SHOOT, I am shooting, ENTER WOMAN, I am entering woman and not even saying anything even if I am not liking it. I am killing everybody, mother, father, grandmother, grandfather, soldier. It is all the same. It is not mattering who it is, just that they are dying. I am thinking thinking. I am thinking that I cannot be doing this anymore.

Then I am getting up from where I am sitting and wiping the mud on my hand onto my short. I am looking at my gun and I am saying to it, I am not needing you anymore. Just stay where you are. My shoulder that it is always sitting on is hurting so much, but I am feeling it jubilating because it is not having to be obeying gun anymore.

Nobody is seeing me as I am getting up and walking through the tree right to the road. I am feeling breezes to my back that is pushing me to walk far far away from here and I am moving quickly quickly onto the road where I am just walking walking walking to where the sun is setting. I am looking at it and wanting to catch it in my hand to be squeezing until the color are dripping out from it forever. That way everywhere it is always dark and nobody is ever having to see any of the terrible thing that is happening in this world.

In heaven, I am thinking it is always morning. It is not mattering when I am waking up, there is always the feeling of warmness from the sunlight that is coming in through the window, and the sound of bird singing outside in the tree, and the sound of the cock shouting KROO KROO, and the smell of smoke coming from where they are making fire. Everything is new. Everything is fresh. That is how I am feeling each time I am waking up in this place.

I am not knowing how long I am staying here, but I am staying here for long time—some week, some month— I am not knowing. All I am knowing is how it is feeling here. From my window, if I am standing on my bed, I can be seeing ocean and hearing how it is just grumbling. And all the time I can be hearing the wind talking when it is blowing through the coconut palm that is standing at tenshun in front of the ocean. Every morning I am getting up and I am going to walk in the sand that is rubbing the skin between my toe until that skin is becoming very red. And every morning I am looking very closely at everything that is here and seeing how crab is running in the sand, and mushroom is growing on the palm-tree truck. Sometimes I am seeing how ant is eating up the coconut that is falling and how new plant is just growing everywhere in this place. When I am seeing this, I am thinking everything is so nice. Everything is so good.

I am not having to worrying about anything from war, like bombing or shelling, or dying. At night we are sleeping inside with fan instead of outside in heat or rain. They are giving us much of food and telling us that we can be sitting down to eating it at the table in room with wall that is painting blue and floor that is just white. They are giving us as much food as we can even be wanting. We are not having to ask if we are wanting more. They are just letting us to take it. Plantain, rice, meats, chicken, fishes—anything we are wanting we are having. Sometimes I am eating even if I am not hungrying too much because I am fearing that the food is finishing and I will not be eating any for the next day.

Now I am strong again. My arm and my leg is carrying me again and when I am walking my bone is not cracking and the whole place is not spinning around and around anymore. I am wearing new clothe—one new shirt that is white with black stripe across my chest and new trouser that is blue and fitting me well well. I am liking it very much because it is clean and dry and it is not having any hole from bullet or blood from the last person who is wearing it. When I am finishing my bath in the morning, I am rushing rushing to be putting on my clothe so everybody can be seeing how I am looking so fine when I am wearing them.

They are giving me one room for myself where I am having whole bed, and my own table right under the window for the sunlight to be warming. They are giving me all of the book I can be wanting to read because I am telling Amy that my father is schoolteacher and that before the war I am always reading whatever I can. They are even giving me as much paper as I can be wanting and telling me to write or draw whatever I am wanting to draw so I am drawing picture of school so I can be finishing and becoming Doctor and Engineer.

There is priest who is coming every Wednesday and Sunday in his black clothe and white collar. He is calling himself Father Festus so we are calling him that. He is very thin, but he is having fat cheek that is folding on each other and hanging to the ground and nose that is covering his whole mouth. He is always wearing sunglass so I am never seeing his eye. Sometimes I am even wondering if he is having eye. He is saying, turn to God. Pray to the Almighty so he can be forgiving you. Confession and Forgiveness and Resurrection, Father Festus is always saying, these are the only thing you are needing to be giving The Life to your life.

I am always thinking Confession and Forgiveness and Resurrection, I am not knowing what all this word is meaning. They are not making any sense to me anytime he is saying them. The only thing that is making sense to me is memory that I am having of another boy—Strika—sleeping next to me, so close because we are the only people protecting each other from all of the thing trying to kill us. I am remembering sound of people coughing and screaming, and the smell of going to toilet and dead body everywhere. This is the only thing that I am knowing. So, I am asking Father Festus about Confession and Forgiveness and Resurrection and he is saying to me, above all my boy, be having faith in God and trusting in him because he is helping you to understand this thing. Are you having Bible?

Yes I am having Bible, but I am using to be holding my drawing down on my desk so the fan is not throwing them everywhere.

Even if I am not understanding all the thing he is saying, I am still listening because he is saying that God is still alive in this place. I do not know if I am believing him, but I am liking to hear it.

And every day I am talking to Amy. She is white woman from America who is coming here to be helping people like me. Her teeths is too small and her tongue is too big for her mouth so she is speaking through her nose, but her nose is too small so sometimes it is troubling me too much to be hearing what she is saying. Most of the time she is not even saying anything and is sitting across from me in her chair. She is sitting in her chair and I am sitting in my own chair and she is always looking at me like looking at me is going to be helping me. She is telling me to speak speak speak and thinking that my not speaking is because I am like baby. If she is thinking I am baby, then I am not speaking because baby is not knowing how to speak. But every time I am sitting with her I am thinking I am like old man and she is like small girl because I am fighting in war and she is not even knowing what war is.

She is always saying to me, tell me what you are feeling. Tell me what you are thinking. And every day I am telling her the same thing, I am thinking about my future. What is your future, she is asking to me. And I am saying I am seeing myself becoming Doctor or Engineer and making too much money so I am becoming big man and never having to fight war ever again. And sometimes I am telling her, I am hearing bullet and scream in my ear and I am wanting to be dying so I am never hearing it again. I am wanting to lie down on the warm ground with my eye closed and the smell of mud in my nose, just like Strika. I am wanting to feel how the ground is wet all around my body so that if I am sweating, I am feeling like it is the ground sweating through me. And I am wanting to stay in this same place forever, never moving for anything, just waiting waiting until dust is piling on me and grasses is covering me and insect is making their home in the space between my teeths. I am telling her that I am thinking one Iroko tree will be growing from my body, so wide that its trunk is separating night and day, and so tall that its top leaf is tickling the moon until the man living there is smiling.

I am saying to her sometimes, I am not saying many thing because I am knowing too many terrible thing to be saying to you. I am seeing more terrible thing than ten thousand men and I am doing more terrible thing than twenty thousand men. So, if I am saying these thing, then it will be making me to sadding too much and you to sadding too much in this life. I am wanting to be happy in this life because of everything I am seeing. I am just wanting to be happy.

When I am saying all of this, she is just looking at me and I am seeing water in her eye. So I am saying to her, if I am telling this to you it will be making you to think that I am some sort of beast or devil. Amy is never saying anything when I am saying this, but the water is just shining in her eye. And I am saying to her, fine. I am all of this thing. I am all of this thing, but I am also having mother once, and she is loving me.

DATE DUE
